A GIRL AND HER TIGER

A GIRL AND HER TIGER

ZOEY GONG

RED EMPRESS
PUBLISHING

Red Empress Publishing
www.RedEmpressPublishing.com

Cover by Cherith Vaughan
www.CoversbyCherith.com

For my friend Cherith, for her support through this endeavor and her beautiful book covers.

CHAPTER ONE

*P*riya reached up to the top of her mother's closet and pulled the box down, as she had done so many times in her life. She lifted the lid and couldn't help but smile at her first glimpse of the bright red silk inside.

Her grandmother's wedding sari was the most beautiful thing Priya had ever seen. The long red cloth was embellished with gold thread in the most ornate designs. Even though Priya had no plans to marry, it had always been her dream to wear the traditional sari in her own wedding one day. As often as she could, she would steal away to her mother's bedroom and sneak a peek at the dress, especially on days like today when she felt like so much of her own culture was being taken from her.

Priya gasped when she heard shouts from outside and rushed to put the sari back exactly as she had found it. She then went to the window and watched as her mother did her best to control the four young children who were scrambling about her.

"Please, don't push me, young sahib," her mother said to Simon, a boy of twelve. "I don't want to drop the eggs."

"Give them to me," Simon demanded.

"I cannot," Priya's mother, her amma, said. "Cook needs them for your lunch today."

"I want an egg!" a little girl named Elsa said as she grabbed the woman's arm and tugged, nearly causing her to lose her balance. Priya felt annoyance rise up in her chest.

"Please, stop," Amma said with far more patience than Priya could have mustered. "We need to get back to the house now for your lessons."

Simon stood defiantly in front of Amma with his arms crossed, stopping her in her tracks. "I don't want to go back for lessons. Give me the eggs. I need them to teach that worthless fan-puller a lesson. He fell asleep three times last night! He's so lazy!"

Priya thought that people who needed to use other humans to fan them through the night were the definition of lazy, but she stayed put, forcing herself to only watch and clench her fists in private. Her mother had warned her before about yelling at the memsahib's children.

"Simon," Amma said, doing her best to be firm without raising her voice. "You know I don't have a choice. I must take the eggs to Cook, and you must attend your lessons. On your mother's orders. Now, come along." She smiled and waved her hand to try and coax Simon to be on his way, but he didn't budge.

Suddenly, from behind her, Luke, the younger son, ran up and grabbed the egg basket, ripping it from Amma's arm. As she tried to retain hold of the basket, several eggs fell out, smashing on the ground.

Amma's hands flew to her mouth. "Luke! Stop this at once," she hissed. "Your mother will be very angry!"

But the children only laughed.

"Angry with you!" Simon howled. He then snatched the basket of eggs from his younger brother and ran off.

"Simon!" Amma called after him, finally raising her voice. "Return the eggs to me right now!"

Simon turned slowly toward her and pulled an egg out of the basket. He locked eyes with Amma.

"Do not even think about it," she warned. But his choice was already made. Even Priya was surprised to see the hatred in the boy's face for the woman who had nursed him since he was a baby.

Priya could not hold back any longer. She could not sit by and let that cruel, spoiled boy egg her mother. She turned, hitched up her own plain sari, and darted out of the house. By the time she reached the door, Simon was rearing his hand back. Priya ran toward him as fast as she could, but she was not fast enough. She watched as he lurched forward, the egg leaving his hand, arching through the air, and then shattering on her mother's chest, the egg goo splattering her face.

The children all burst into laughter, but Priya was in a rage. She continued running toward Simon, her face hot with fury. He must have heard her running toward him because he turned toward her and his face went white. He raised his arms in front of him to ward off the blow.

"Priya!"

Priya froze only inches from Simon at the sound of her mother's voice.

"Go inside, now!" Amma ordered.

"But," Priya protested, "look what he did."

"And I will let his mother know," Amma said. "She will deal with him."

"You know she won't," Priya said. In all of her life, she

had never known their mother to so much as raise her voice at her children.

"Yeah, go inside, Priya," Simon mocked as he turned and walked away, still holding the basket of eggs and tossing one up and down like a ball. "Before I tell my mother what you almost did and she refuses to speak for you this afternoon." The boys laughed as they wandered away, and Priya fumed. She was so angry over the fact that Simon—and his whole family—held her entire life in their hands. One bad word from the memsahib and Priya would never hope to find a position with a respectable family—even if she didn't want a position anyway.

"Lucille!" Amma called out to the eldest daughter, who had just come outside to see what the commotion was about.

Lucille, with her blue eyes and curly blonde hair, bounded down the stairs and across the green lawn.

"Goodness me, amah," Lucille said with a chuckle to Priya's mother, using the preferred British term for a nanny. "What happened to you?"

"Your brothers," Priya grumbled. Lucille only nodded knowingly.

"Can you take your sisters inside so I may go change?" Priya's mother asked Lucille.

"Of course," Lucille said, reaching for her sisters' hands. "I'll see you later, Priya! I can't wait."

Priya only wrinkled her nose but didn't respond as she took her mother's hand and led her into the house.

"If you are going to be an amah yourself," her mother said once they were indoors, "you need to learn to have more patience."

Priya sighed as she helped her mother undress and

place the soiled clothes into a wash bin. "I need to learn patience, and those children need to learn respect."

"Children are children," Amma interrupted. "You spit at me more than once when you were little."

"But I'm your daughter!" Priya said. "I would never treat another woman that way. You raised me better than that."

"And the Parker children will grow out of it, eventually," Amma said. "Is not Lucille Parker like a sister to you?"

Priya sighed and shook her head. "When we were younger, perhaps, since you practically raised both of us. But ever since she went to school, she has changed."

"Lucille is the same girl she ever was," Priya's mother said. "Spoiled, high-strung. More worried about boys and dresses than anything else. I think you are the one who changed."

"Maybe," Priya said. "It isn't fair that she got to go to that fancy academy while I had to endure lectures about how great it has been to be part of the British Empire by a bunch of sour-faced nuns."

"We *are* fortunate to be part of such a mighty empire," Amma said, growing exasperated. "If it were not for the British, we could have been overrun by some other military power that didn't have our best interests at heart."

"We could have defended ourselves," Priya countered.

"And we have advancements in railroads and medicine and—" Amma went on.

"Which we could have developed too," Priya interrupted.

"To be part of British culture and heritage is a great honor," Amma said.

"Indian culture is older!" Priya said. "What about our heritage? Our history? I'm not British. I'm Indian!"

"Priya!" Amma snapped. "That is enough. We can't

change the past. We are here, now, and we have to make the best life we can. The British rule India, and you need to find your place here. We don't have enough money for a dowry, so you cannot marry. The Parkers' children are growing up, so they are cutting down on staff. You need to find a good placement of your own so you can earn money and a place in society. No amount of grumbling will change that."

"I'm not grumbling," Priya grumbled. "It is no small thing to be treated like you are less than dirt in your own country."

"That is enough!" Amma finally yelled. "Go to your room and get dressed. Memsahib Parker is taking us to meet the Evans family in an hour. You will wear the dress that Lucille gave you and you will smile and nod and you will get that position. Do you understand me?"

Priya pressed her lips to keep from being disrespectful to her mother, but she didn't understand how her parents could be so accepting of the British. Of course her mother didn't publicly speak against them because she didn't want to lose her job. But in private, did her mother truly believe that the way things were was the best way to live? Wasn't she even a tiny bit resentful of the way she—and all Indians —were treated? Priya had spent her entire life watching the Parker family walk all over her mother and father. As a child, she too just accepted it. But as she grew older, she grew to despise how the British treated her parents, and everyone else.

But Priya knew that what her mother said held a grain of truth. What else could Priya do? She couldn't go to a university. She couldn't get married. Even if she did marry, her husband would be at the employ of some British man or family. She had to earn money somehow to support herself and contribute to the family, and the only openings for women were as amahs. They were coveted positions, ones that paid well. She *should* be grateful that Memsahib Parker was making an introduction for Priya to the Evans family. Countless other Indian girls would kill for such an advantage. But Priya hated that her very existence was in the hands of a foreign family. She felt as if her life was not her own. As if she lived simply to be at the whim of snobbish British women and their rude children.

But her mother was right. What could she do about it?

So Priya bit her tongue and nodded her head. "Yes, Amma." But she didn't head straight to her room. She went to the garden instead, hoping that a walk might clear her head and cool her temper. After all, it wasn't Amma she was angry at.

She was angry at everyone and everything else. She crossed her arms as she walked through the lush garden of the Parker estate where Priya and her family lived. Since both of Priya's parents worked for the Parkers, they were allowed to live in a small house on the estate. Many other servants lived on the estate as well, but most of them shared another small house while some lived in the attic of the main house. The Parkers had at least fifteen servants at any given time, and they did everything for the Parkers, from raising their children to fanning them while they slept. To most Indians, the Parkers were of the highest class and ridiculously wealthy. But she had heard once that by British standards, the Parkers were not very well-off. Back in England, they could barely afford a cook and a maid, much less an entire staff. Priya wondered what it was about living in India that allowed such mediocre people like the Parkers to live like kings, but that was an aspect of life she didn't understand, and probably never would. She was Indian with a very basic British education. She could read and write English, do basic math, and could name all the British monarchs from the last one hundred years. She could also speak Hindi, but that was about the extent of her knowledge about the world. She knew the world had more to offer, but she didn't know how to reach it. She didn't want to be just a servant, and eventually just a wife. In truth, she only knew what she *didn't* want. She had no idea what she wanted instead because she didn't know what opportunities existed. It was as though she was going through life in a fog. She knew *something* was out there, something just beyond her field of vision, but she didn't know what it was. She only had a feeling that whatever it was, it was better than what she had now.

"Priya!" she heard a voice yell as a hand grabbed her arm. Priya gasped and looked over. "Are you sleepwalking?" Lucille asked.

"Sorry," Priya said. "I was just thinking."

Lucille nodded. "Today is a big day for you!" she said, a huge grin on her face. "If you get that position with the Evans family, I'll be able to visit you all the time! It will be as if you never left."

Priya wrinkled her nose. "Do you really think Memsahib Evans will let you fraternize with her servant?"

"Oh, come now," Lucille said, her blue eyes sparkling. "It won't be as bad as all that. Amahs are like family. You know I adore your mother."

Priya cocked her head. "What family members do you throw eggs at?"

Lucille gasped. "W-w-what?"

"What family members have you torn their clothes and then laughed about it?" Priya went on, recalling an event from a few years ago.

Lucille crossed her arms. "That was Simon, not me."

"You laughed," Priya reminded her.

"We were just kids," Lucille said. "We all do naughty things when we are little."

"I never disrespected your mother," Priya said.

"So, you think you're better than me?" Lucille asked sharply.

"I didn't say that," Priya said. "I'm just saying that we aren't family."

"How can you be so mean?" Lucille said. "You know, I knew that you were pulling away from me. I've barely seen you or spoken to you in weeks. I thought you were just busy. I had no idea it was because you were such a jerk!"

"I'm just stating the facts," Priya said. "You are the one calling names."

"Here is a fact," Lucille said. "I thought you were like a sister to me! I gave you the dress for your presentation today."

"Ugh, that corseted monstrosity that I can't breathe in?" Priya asked, rolling her eyes. "I'd rather wear a sari!"

"And my mother loves you," Lucille went on. "That is why she is going out of her way to introduce you to Mrs. Evans!"

"Oh yes," Priya said. "It is such a hassle to cross the street and talk over tea and crumpets!"

Lucille's mouth gaped, but Priya didn't care. She raised her chin and dared Lucille to keep arguing with her. It was true that Priya had once considered Lucille her best friend. But their lives had taken dramatically different courses lately, and Priya resented it greatly. She had tried to keep her feelings to herself instead of lashing out at Lucille. But with the real threat of her having to follow her mother's footsteps now only moments away, she couldn't keep it contained any longer.

"You know, I was going to go with you today," Lucille said. "So I could tell Mrs. Evans how wonderful you are. But I think I'll just stay home."

"Fine. I'd hate for you to go 'out of your way' to do something for a family member," Priya mocked.

"You are so frustrating!" Lucille said as she growled and stomped her foot before turning and walking away.

Priya sighed and headed back home. The walk had done little to clear her head, and probably made her feel more upset. But what could she do? Her mother would never forgive her if she didn't at least try to get the amah position with the Evans family. It was time for her to get dressed and face her future, no matter how miserable it might make her.

CHAPTER TWO

*P*riya held her breath as her mother stood behind her and pulled the strings of her corset tight. British women didn't usually like Indian women adopting British styles, as though their clothing was sacred and belonged only to them. But for a new family just arrived from England like the Evans, having a possible nanny who was somewhat Anglicized was usually seen in a positive light. They would want to make sure that the woman tasked with raising their children would instill in them British morals and standards. So, for now, Priya was expected to attend the introduction in British dress. If she got the position, she could then return to dressing in her sari.

The dress was not the most hideous one Priya had ever seen. It was a simple blue dress with an even darker blue pattern. With Priya's black hair and dark skin, she thought she might be able to blend into the shadows and go unseen for most of the afternoon. Even though she was the reason for the entire afternoon event, she knew from experience that after the initial introductions, the British people would probably forget she and her mother were even there.

The dress only required one crinoline underneath to fill out the skirt, and it blessedly had short sleeves. Most of the time, Priya wondered how British women didn't fall over dead in their layers of clothes and tight corsets in the oppressive Indian summers. She donned a simple straw bonnet with a matching blue ribbon and grabbed a lace parasol as she followed her mother out the door.

"Oh, Priya!" Memsahib Parker gasped when she saw her. "Aren't you just pretty as a picture."

"Thank you, ma'am," Priya said.

"Lucille," Memsahib Parker said, nudging her daughter out from behind her. "That dress compliments Priya's coloring so well!"

Priya paused and looked at Lucille with surprise. Lucille sighed and looked at her nails and then up at the sun, anywhere but at Priya.

"I guess," Lucille said.

Priya's anger softened. She was touched that Lucille had changed her mind and decided to join their little expedition across the road. Priya offered her a little smile, which Lucille finally saw, and she smiled back. They didn't need to use words to reassure each other that they were friends again.

"It's...nice," Priya said. "Thank you."

"Are we ready?" Memsahib Parker asked, and the rest of the women nodded. "Good," she said and led them like ducks in a row out a side gate and down the road toward the Evans' home.

As Priya looked up and down the street of elegant British-style houses, she wondered for a moment if she wasn't in the center of Bombay at all but had been transported to London. Even though she had been raised in the British neighborhood, she had never felt at home here. She preferred visiting her aunts and uncles and cousins in a nearby village where the sights and smells were distinctly Indian.

"I hear that little Simon was being quite a scamp this morning," Memsahib Parker said to Amma.

"Yes, ma'am," she replied. "Ruined the whole basket of eggs."

"Well, I did let him know that he shouldn't have done that," Memsahib Parker replied. "You'll just have to go to the market later and get more."

"Of course, ma'am," Amma said, and Priya cursed to herself. Going to the market was no small feat, as Memsahib Parker made it sound. The eggs that Simon had destroyed were from the Parkers' own coop. But the market was nearly an hour's walk away. And at the end of the day, nearly all the best eggs would be gone, if there were any left at all.

"Perhaps Cook could make something else," Priya offered. "Something that didn't require eggs."

"Oh, but it is Thursday!" Memsahib cried, as if that made a difference. "She needs to prepare the cakes for this weekend or we won't have time to have the sweets prepared for luncheon on Saturday."

"Then perhaps Simon could go to the market since Simon was the one who destroyed the eggs," Priya offered.

"Send a child into the dangerous streets of Bombay?" Memsahib Parker asked, her hand flying to her chest in horror. "I do hope you are joking, Priya! You are applying to be an amah! Have you no care?"

Priya nearly opened her mouth to declare that she wasn't joking and that is wasn't fair for her mother to be punished for Simon's actions, but her mother grabbed her arm to stop her.

"Of course she is kidding, aren't you, Priya?" she said as she squeezed Priya's arm in such a way that brooked no argument.

"Of course, Amma," Priya said, dropping her head to her chest.

"When it comes to children, we must always be flexible, patient, and forgiving," Amma said. "And I have taught Priya this too."

Memsahib smiled with a sigh and nodded. "That is why you are the best amah we could have asked for," she said. "And why I am so honored to help Priya get this position with Mrs. Evans. Won't it be nice having Priya so close?"

"It is indeed a blessing," Amma said, and Priya only nodded. She was grateful that she would be so near to her mother, even if she would hardly have a chance to see her again. The only time an amah had time for herself to visit friends or family or even do a bit of shopping was just one half-day a month. She knew that if she did get the position with the Evans family, she was going to miss her parents terribly, even if they were living only down the street.

They turned down a side path next to one of the largest houses on the street and went through a gate into the back garden. There, several British men and women were sitting and standing around talking and laughing. Over to one side near a well were several children playing with some kittens. Priya was horrified to see that one of the boys was holding a kitten precariously at the well's edge, looking deep into the dark cavern.

"Please! Be careful!" Priya admonished the child, jutting away from her mother toward the boy.

"Priya!" Amma hissed, and Priya stopped in her tracks.

Priya looked around and noticed that everyone was watching her, as though waiting to see what she would do. She forced a smile to her face and calmed her voice.

"Sweet little one," Priya said. "Please, be careful. We don't want anyone to fall in."

"I know what I'm doing!" the little boy barked back as he returned to looking over the edge.

Priya's heart was beating so hard she could feel it in her nose as she heard the kitten whimpering. The mother cat was also pacing nervously nearby as she watched all her kittens in the hands of the children.

"There," Memsahib Parker said. "Isn't Priya so good with children, and animals?" She chuckled and the rest of the garden party guests did too.

Priya grimace and forced herself to turn away from the children. She knew that if she wanted to make a good impression, she needed to ignore any of their bad behavior today. But once she was their amah, treating animals with kindness was going to be a top lesson for her to impart to her young charges.

She was surprised at how many people were there. She had thought the tea would only be with Sahib and Memsahib Evans and their children. But they seemed to have invited all of their friends as well. Two of the British people walked over and greeted Memsahib Parker while the others all took their seats.

"Priya," Memsahib Parker said, "this is Mr. and Mrs. Evans."

"Pleased to meet you," Priya said with a small curtsey.

"Excellent manners," Memsahib Evans said to Memsahib Parker, as though Priya couldn't hear her. "I was so worried about what it would be like having foreign staff. Would they have any manners at all? How would we communicate? I'm so glad to have a friend like you here to help us get settled."

"The Company instituted British education years ago," Priya said. "We all speak English." She could almost feel her mother groan at her words.

The Evans looked at Priya as if she had insulted them, but Lucille spoke up.

"Priya's mother has worked for my mother since before she was born," she explained. "If you need someone in your household who knows how things are done and can help you with any aspect of life here in India, no one would be better for you than Priya."

"So true!" Memsahib Parker said, patting her daughter on the arm and rushing in to diffuse the situation. "Any family who hires Priya will be getting so much more than an amah. Shall we sit down and discuss the placement further?"

"Oh, how rude of me!" Memsahib Evans said as she led them to some seats around a small table that was already laid out with tea and various small sweets and sandwiches. "Please, have a seat and some tea."

Sahib Evans then went around and introduced the other couples to Memsahib Parker. They were all relatively new to Bombay and in need of an amah. If the Evans did not take a liking to Priya, one of the other families was sure to. This was indeed an enviable position to be in. There was very little chance of Priya leaving this tea without a position. A notion that made Priya nervous, but she knew it made her mother glad. Priya did her best to bite her tongue and be on her best behavior so she could make her mother proud.

"I simply don't know how you do it, Susan," Memsahib Evans said to Memsahib Parker. "I have only been here a few days and am so out of my element I feel on the edge of tears at every moment. But to be here for years on end! To raise your children here! How do you do it?"

"One must simply grow where they are planted," Memsahib Parker said sagely. "We are here in this strange and foreign land and must adapt."

It is not strange or foreign to me, Priya thought but did not say.

"And we are so lucky to have the Company here," Memsahib Parker went on. "They really can import anything you need. It just takes a bit of planning. You'll see. After a few weeks, you'll get used to the way things are here."

"Oh, I don't think I ever could get used to it," Memsahib Evans said. "This heat is just unbearable. The smells are offensive! The way we were hustled and jostled about at the port, it was so crowded! It was terrifying. I almost got back on the ship and sailed for home right then!"

"She nearly did," Sahib Evans said with a laugh, and the other men joined in.

"Women simply aren't as well-suited for adventure," one of the other men said.

If only they would just leave their dreadful wives at home then, Priya thought as she let her eyes wander back over the yard toward the children she would have to mind if she were given the position of amah.

She gasped as she saw the boy from earlier push a little girl. The little girl shoved him back, into the edge of the stone wall of the well. His hand flew up, knocking the kitten he had been playing with earlier down the shaft.

"Stop!" Priya yelled as she jumped up and ran across the yard.

"What is it?" Memsahib Evans cried out, jumping up. "The children!"

The other parents all began fussing as they followed behind Priya.

"Please, please, please," Priya prayed as she pushed the boy aside. She hoped the kitten had landed in a bucket or on a stone sticking out of the side of the well. Maybe the well was dry and the kitten had landed safely. Anything.

"What's wrong?" Sahib Evans asked, picking up his son who was now crying from being pushed.

"Priya!" her mother called. "What's happening?"

"Be quiet!" Priya yelled over the noise. Her heart froze as she heard pitiful mewling and splashing from deep in the well. "Oh no! Hurry! Someone! Bring a bucket!"

"I'm sure there is nothing we can do," one of the men said. "If you drop a bucket, it will only push the poor thing under the water."

"Might be the merciful thing to do," someone else said.

"Then bring a rope, a branch!" Priya said as she moved around the well, trying to get a better look down to see if there was any hope of rescuing the kitten. "A small log it can grab onto. Anything!"

"Priya," her mother said, pulling her away from the well. "There's nothing we can do."

They all stood around helplessly as the mewling eventually stopped. The mother cat jumped up on the edge of the well and began pacing, meowing for her kitten.

"Well, that was a rather dreadful thing to happen," said one of the men as he led his wife back to the seats.

The boy was still crying in Sahib Evans's arms.

"Don't worry, son," Sahib Evans said. "We'll get you another kitten. A better one."

"Are you joking?" Priya spat. "You would reward that hideous behavior with another animal for your little monster to kill?"

"Priya!" Amma hissed, but Priya did not back down. She simply stared at Sahib Evans, his eyes wide in shock.

"The only monster here is *you*," Memsahib Evans said as she took her son from her husband's arms. "How dare you speak to your betters, your *prospective employer*, in such a manner!"

"You might be prospective employers," Priya said. "But you are *not* my betters. I would never treat animals, or humans—" She shot Memsahib Parker a look. "—as badly as your children do."

"Well!" Memsahib Evans said. "I think this interview is at an end." With that, she turned on her heels and stomped out of the garden.

"Priya," Amma said, shaking her arm. "Go home."

Priya looked around at all the angry faces, especially that of Memsahib Parker. Even Lucille was shaking her head in disgust.

"I...I'm sorry, Amma—" she started to say, but she interrupted her.

"Now!"

Priya hated leaving her mother there to clean up the mess she had made, but she knew that she could not make things right. She turned and ran for home.

CHAPTER THREE

"Have you lost your mind?" Priya's father, her appa, bellowed that night when he got home. He had been with Sahib Parker all day, negotiating with some Indian merchants. But as soon as he arrived home, he had heard about Priya's disastrous interview with the Evans. "It was one thing—even a noble thing—to try and rescue the kitten. But to insult the child? And insult the Evans's parenting? What were you thinking?"

"I don't know, Appa!" Priya bawled. "It was just so awful! Their children were so rude. And the kitten! You should have heard how pitiful—"

"I don't want to hear about it," Appa said. "You know what will be pitiful? The cries you make in the night over your starving belly because you can't get a job. Did you think of that?"

"Of course...after..." Priya said. "That's why I apologized."

"Apologized," Appa scoffed. "I know you did. To the Parkers. To the Evans. To the Evans children. But do you think Memsahib Evans will ever let you anywhere near her children? Or the other mothers who were there today? Not a single family will offer you a position now."

Priya felt tears welling up in her eyes, but she was determined not to cry. Not yet. Not in front of her parents.

"You are lucky your amma and I even have jobs after that," Appa continued to rail. "Do you know what your amma had to do to make sure we still had a roof over her head tonight? How she had to get down on her knees and beg forgiveness. How she had to take the blame as a poor and worthless mother."

"She's not!" Priya said as her shame was quickly replaced with a familiar anger. "She's not a bad mother. Those memsahibs are bad mothers."

"It doesn't matter, Priya!" Appa yelled. "In this world, we do what we must to survive. If we didn't have these jobs, there are a hundred, a thousand other people waiting to take our places. And now you are at the bottom of that list. It will take a natural disaster, a flood, an earthquake. A great death of all of our countrymen in order for you to ever have a chance at a job again."

"Don't say such things," Amma finally said, stepping forward.

Appa ran his fingers through his hair and stepped away. "Ahhh. I know. I'm just...so angry. So disappointed. How could this happen?"

"Your daughter," Amma said, looking at Priya with a tenderness that made Priya want to weep. "She is heart soft. She feels everything so deeply. So personally. It was as though she could feel the terror the kitten felt. She could see nothing else and lashed out in fear."

Priya's mouth gaped a little. She had thought she had lashed out in anger. Anger was her old friend. A feeling that burned inside her at almost every waking moment when she considered the unfair world she lived in. But not for the first time, her mother knew her even better than she knew herself. As she thought back to what had happened in the garden, she realized her mother was right. She had felt anger, yes, but there was a twinge of fear there as well. Not to mention heartbreak, for the kitten and its mother. She had felt so many things, but fear was certainly there.

"She needs to toughen up," Appa said. "Does she think life is going to be easier now?"

"I know it won't be," Priya dared to say. "I'm sorry, Appa. I don't know what else to do or say."

"Well, we better find out soon," Appa said, crossing the room and plopping down on an old chair. He rubbed his face and let out a sigh. "What are any of us going to do? We don't have the money for a dowry. You could marry, but any man who would have you would be so poor...I don't want to imagine the difficult life you would have."

Priya nodded and dared to move from the kneeling position she had been in for the last twenty minutes in front of her father to the more comfortable one of sitting on a nearby stool. Her father's anger seemed to have cooled. He had moved from yelling to problem-solving. This was not the first crisis they had ever faced as a family. But they had always come through their problems together.

"But if she married a farmer," Amma suggested, taking a seat in a nearby rocking chair, "at least then she would not go hungry."

"Until the next drought or famine," Appa said, shaking his head.

"Fine," Amma said. "We will forego any attempt at a marriage, for now. But what about a job? What will she do now?"

"Finding her a placement here in Bombay..." Appa shook his head. "But maybe Goa, or Calcutta."

"Calcutta is so far!" Priya wanted to cry. Calcutta was on the complete other side of the country. If she were sent there, she would probably never see her parents again. Even Goa was bad enough as far south as it was.

"We don't have a lot of options," Appa said. "The problem will still be introductions. We don't know many people in either place."

"If we wait a couple of weeks, Memsahib Parker might forget all about the incident and agree to write a letter of introduction for her," Amma said. "We could use a placement agency to find openings."

"Those places charge a fee," Priya reminded them. "A hefty one."

"Well, the children are all in school now for a large part of the day. I could take in some washing and sewing. Earn the fees that way."

"Amma! No!" Priya said. "I can't have you work even more to pay for the mess I have put us in!"

Amma shook her head and looked at Priya with pity. "My dear little tiger. That is what parents do. We sacrifice all for our children."

"I won't let you!" Priya said, jumping to her feet and running to the door.

"Where are you going?" Amma asked.

"I...I don't know," Priya said. "But I'm going to figure this out!" She left the little house before her parents could stop her. She didn't know where she was going to go or what she was going to do, but she couldn't just sit around any longer. She needed to do something. She needed to at least go for a walk, clear her head.

She walked toward the main house, which lit up the

night like a lantern. She looked up into one of the windows and saw Lucille brushing out her hair. She looked angelic, her golden halo glowing in the dark.

Priya both loved and hated Lucille. Lucille was spoiled, yes, but she was kind and funny. When they were girls, they had pinky swore to always be there for each other. But as they got older, more and more doors opened for Lucille, while more and more closed on Priya. Lucille could do anything she wanted. She could marry or go to university. She could stay in India or go back to England. She could open her own business here in India or be a memsahib like her mother. But for Priya, she only ever had two options— marriage or servitude. And now even those options were closed to her.

At a loss for what else to do, Priya silently slipped up the steps to the back porch. Then she walked over to the gable that held the creeping roses and climbed up it. Once she was on the overhanging for the second floor, she inched along the wall until she reached Lucille's window. She tapped on it and heard a gasp from inside. She waved, and a moment later the window flew open and Lucille reached her hand out. Priya grabbed it and jumped into the room.

"Priya!" Lucille whispered loudly. "What are you doing here?"

Priya straightened herself and smoothed out her sari. "I was just out for a walk and thought I would stop by. For old times' sake."

"Hmm," Lucille said, cocking her eyebrow. "Old times indeed. I can't remember the last time you snuck in here."

Priya shrugged her shoulders. She couldn't either. But it had been a while. When Priya was little, her mother would put her to bed and then have to go back to the main house to tend to the Parker babies overnight. Priya would get scared and lonely, so she would sneak out and climb into Lucille's bedroom where they would laugh and play until they passed out. At first light, Priya would sneak back home, her mother never the wiser. But after the children were old enough to sleep through the night, Amma was able to spend the night in her own home, so Priya's nighttime visits to Lucille were curtailed.

"Do you want to talk about today?" Lucille asked.

"Not really," Priya said. "It was pretty terrible."

"You aren't kidding," Lucille said. "After you left, Mrs. Evans wouldn't stop railing about how insufferable it would be to have Indian servants. Her husband was trying to keep things under control, but he was furious. Apparently, it was hard enough convincing the woman to come here and now he's afraid she is just going to run back home, even though there is no way they could afford it."

"Why do such women even bother coming?" Priya asked. "They are miserable here and they make everyone else miserable as well. Just stay in your own country!"

"They are families," Lucille said with a shrug. "They want to be together. I can't imagine going back to England and leaving my parents back here."

"My parents are talking about sending me to Goa, or Calcutta," Priya said sadly. "They are afraid I won't find a job here in Bombay."

"That's terrible!" Lucille said. "We'd never see each other again!"

Priya nodded, even though not seeing Lucille hadn't even crossed her mind before now. She had been rather indifferent to the possibility, but now, in the presence of her friend, she realized that she would miss her too.

"We don't know what else to do," Priya said. "No one in Bombay will hire me."

"No one who is *staying* in Bombay will hire you," Lucille said, a mischievous smile crossing her face.

"What do you mean?" Priya asked.

"I overheard my papa talking to one of his business associates a few days ago," Lucille said as she went to her desk and pulled out a pen and piece of paper. "His name was Lord Fullerton. He's an exporter. He said that there is a need for Indian women overseas. But they only stay for a few years."

"What do you mean?" Priya asked. "What kind of need? Why do they only stay a few years?"

"I don't know exactly," Lucille said. "Servants I guess. Servants in England make a lot more money than servants here. I think they earn so much money, they don't have to work for long and then they come back home."

"There are Indian servants in England?" Priya asked.

Lucille shrugged. "The last time I was there, many families had India servants they had taken back with them. Maybe having Indian servants is becoming fashionable."

Priya chuffed at the idea of being a fashion statement, but the possibility of being a servant in England, and making a lot of money in the process, certainly held some appeal. She hated the idea of being sent to Calcutta, but even living there, she would never see her parents again. She could never earn enough money to come home. England might be further away, but if she could earn enough money to come back home, and have money to spare, it might be worth it.

"Where can I find Lord Fullerton?" Priya asked.

Lucille tore off the piece of paper and handed it to her. "It's a little far. Probably dangerous at night to get there. But you could go tomorrow morning. I could even go with you!"

Priya looked at the paper. The address was another

British neighborhood a few miles away. It would be dangerous to try and get there at night, but Priya was anxious to meet this man and find out what he could do for her. She didn't want to waste a moment. If she could make arrangements to travel to England and have good news for her parents in the morning about her future, then they wouldn't have to worry anymore.

Priya clutched the paper to her chest and then squeezed Lucille's hand. "Yes," she said. "In the morning. Thank you, my dear friend."

Lucille beamed and pulled Priya in for a hug. Priya sighed and hugged her friend back. When Lucille finally let her go, Priya went back to the window and slipped back down to the garden. Once she was safe back on the grass, Lucille waved at her and then pulled her curtain shut. Then, instead of heading back home, Priya went out a side gate and into the dark streets of the city.

CHAPTER FOUR

As Priya slipped out the side gate, her heart beat fast in her chest. She had never ventured outside of the estate's gates at night before. It was far too dangerous for a girl to be out alone. As soon as she heard the gate lock click behind her, she turned around and tried to pull it back open. This was a mistake! But the gate was locked, and from this side of the house, there was no way back inside without knocking on the front door, which she wasn't about to do. She could not face Sahib and Memsahib Parker after the events of the day.

She took a few deep breaths and put one foot in front of the other. In only a few steps, she was at the street. This neighborhood was not particularly frightening. There were lamps along the street and it was rather quiet. All the houses had lights burning inside them, which gave the street a warm glow. There were a few Indian people out, working in the front yards or walking pet dogs for their sahibs, but for the most part, the street was deserted. At the far end of the street, she could see two British men in uniform. They served as night watchmen to keep the neighborhood secure. Priya slipped down the street in the opposite direction, staying to the shadows. She didn't want to risk being seen and dragged back home. When she got to the end of the road, she turned left and kept walking.

It didn't take long for the atmosphere to completely change. The street got noisy and crowded as she stepped into a bustling night market. She was surprised to see so many people out. Men, women, and even children. Though no one seemed to be alone. The children were in groups and accompanied by at least one parent, and the women were all in the company of men. Priya rubbed her arms and moved quickly, avoiding eye contact.

The street was filthy, and she could feel moisture seeping through the soft soles of her shoes, but she kept walking. She passed a house with several women in beautiful shining saris hanging about and calling to the men nearby. The smoke and spices from the food stalls threatened to cloud her eyes. Everyone shouted at each other as they tried to hawk their wares. After a while, Priya couldn't help but slow her steps as some beautiful necklaces and shoes caught her eye.

"Pretty trinkets for a pretty girl!" a man called out to her. She shook her head and kept walking.

"What are you doing out so late, pretty girl?" another man called from a stall across the way.

Priya turned away and quickened her steps again. She realized she had left the house without anything. No money, no identification. If someone tried to rob her, they would be sorely disappointed. If she were killed, there would be no way to identify her body. As her heart beat hard in her chest, she walked faster. Why had she left the house at night? She was so stupid.

"Hey, girl!" someone called out. She had no idea if the

man was calling to her or not. She didn't stop to see. She took off at a full run, her long braid flowing behind her.

She turned down a side alley and kept running. She could see the end of the market just ahead, and then it would be only a few blocks to the British neighborhood where Lord Fullerton lived. But then she felt someone grab her arm and jerk her backward. She screamed but a hand covered her mouth.

"Hey, pretty girl," the man said, his breath hot on her ear. "No need to scream."

She raised her knee and it connected with the man's groin. He grunted and loosened his grip. She was able to slip away from him and through a market stall. The family working there seemed surprised, but she kept running. She darted from one stall to another, from one aisle to the next. Some people tried to stop her, but whether they wanted to help her or assault her, she had no idea. She wormed her way out of their grasps and finally out of the market completely. She ran into a wooded area and hid among the shrubs and shadows while she caught her breath. She was scared and knew she had made a wrong choice. She never should have left home alone at night. She should have waited until the morning. But now, returning home would mean going back through the crowded marketplace and knocking on the front door of the house to get inside. She pulled the address for Lord Fullerton out of her pocket. She was closer to her destination than to her home. There was no going back now. If she could just get to Lord Fullerton's and make arrangements, then he could help her get back home to say goodbye to her parents. She shored up her courage, took a deep breath, and got back to her feet.

Soon, she was in the British neighborhood where she should be able to find Lord Fullerton's house. It was much later now, and the night was pitch black. There were no people milling about, save for a few night watchmen. She darted from yard to yard and from tree to tree to avoid the guards. She wasn't sure which house she was looking for, so she had to look at the numbers on each one to try and find the right house.

She screamed when she ended up too close to a dog in one of the yards. The dog barked furiously and charged toward her. She ran to the street, but thankfully the dog was stopped by a chain around his neck. But as she turned, she saw two of the night watchmen running toward her with their guns raised. She knew better than to try and run. The men would most certainly shoot her and then ask questions later. She raised her hands and lowered her eyes.

"I'm lost," she said pitifully as the guards reached her.

"Who are you?" one of the men demanded.

"My name is Priya," she said. No sense in lying. She didn't need to tell them the whole truth, just enough to get her where she needed to go. "I...I was running an errand for Lord Fullerton and lost track of the time. I'm just trying to get home."

"You work for Lord Fullerton?" one of the men asked.

"I...I can show you," she said. The men nodded and she slowly reached her hand into her pocket and pulled out the paper with Lord Fullerton's address. It wasn't anything official, but there were scant reasons why she would have the address in her pocket. She handed the paper to one of the guards, who snatched it out of her hand.

"She does appear to have been heading to Martin's house," the man said to his companion.

"Right," the second man said, lowering his rifle. "It's dangerous out here for a maid, don't you know?"

"I know," she said humbly. "I'm heading inside right now."

"We'll escort you," the first man said, gripping her arm.

She nodded her thanks, glad that they would take her to the right house. But how would Lord Fullerton react? He wouldn't know her or be expecting her. She had to think fast.

One of the guards knocked on the door and an Indian butler opened it.

"This girl says she's lost," the guard told him.

"Yes?" the butler asked, confused.

"I was sent by Lord Fullerton to see Sahib Parker," Priya interjected.

The butler looked even more confused.

"Is Lord Fullerton at home?" the guard asked. "We just want to make sure everything is on the up and up."

The butler gave a polite bow and ducked into the house. A moment later, a tall white man with silver hair and a full beard holding a brandy glass appeared.

"What's all this then, good sirs?" he asked.

"This young lady says she belongs to you, m'lord," one of the guards said.

"Does she?" Fullerton said, cocking an eyebrow at her. Priya dared to look him in the eye with a pleading look. Apparently, his curiosity got the better of him and he gave a laugh. "Of course she does! I had forgotten for a moment. You know, all these darkie servants look the same at first glance. Get in here, girl. You're quite late."

Priya ripped her arm from the guard and slipped inside the house. She heard Fullerton thank the guards and then shut the door behind her. At first, she was in awe of the house. It was far more grand and well-apportioned than the Parker house. The Parker house had once been an Indian house, but it had been modified to be more British. They added rugs and wall-hangings, but the house still felt cobbled together. This house seemed to have been built from the ground up in the British style. While the Parkers had always seemed rich, this man felt like true wealth. She had never considered that there could be a difference before now.

"So, to what do I owe the pleasure of this surprise visit...?" Fullerton asked.

"Priya," she offered. "My name is Priya."

"Priya," Fullerton repeated and then sipped from his glass, never taking his eyes off of her. Priya felt her skin crawl, but she did not avert her gaze. She had come here to ask for a job. She needed to show confidence.

"Priya," he said again and motioned with his hand down a hallway. "Please, join me in my study." He then turned and led the way, taking for granted that she would follow him.

He stopped at a room and slid the doors open, revealing a room of dark wood and rich colors. The walls were lined with books and a large desk sat to one side. The stuffed carcass of a tiger lunging forward with her claws extended and fangs bared was situated in one corner.

"I shot that myself," Fullerton said when he saw her eyes linger on the tiger. She gave a small smile to hide her disdain. She did not understand the British obsession with hunting trophies. While Indians hunted for food and some-times had to kill a tiger that was a danger to a village, they did not hunt for sport. While not all Hindus were vegetar-ian, it was a sacred duty to inflict as little pain on the world as possible.

"Would you care for a drink?" Fullerton offered her a brandy glass. She shook her head. "Very well," he said and he motioned for the butler who Priya had not heard follow them into the room. "Tea for Miss Priya."

"Sir," the man said as he bowed out of the room.

"So," Fullerton said as he sat behind his desk and motioned for her to take a seat across from him. "What can I do for you? You mentioned something about Parker?"

Priya decided to fudge the truth a bit to increase her chances of getting a job. "Sahib Parker said that you have jobs, opportunities for Indian girls overseas."

This seemed to peek Fullerton's attention. The butler returned and placed a tea tray on a table.

"That will do, Arjun," he said and quickly ushered the butler out of the room, sliding the door shut behind him. He then went over and prepared a cup of tea for Priya himself.

"No thank you," she said when he offered her the cup. "I don't want to be a bother."

"It's no bother," he said, pushing the cup into her hand. "And I insist."

She gave a small smile and sipped at the tea, which was actually quite good. "Thank you," she whispered.

Fullerton then sat on the edge of his desk near her. "So, you've come to me to find...work of some sort overseas. You must be in a hell of a lot of trouble."

Priya gulped more of her tea. How could he know? Well, of course, only girls who were out of options in India would even consider taking a job in another country.

"I...I was stupid," she admitted. "I made a mistake. Ruined my chance at getting a position with a good family and my parents are too poor for a dowry."

"Was it a boy?" Fullerton asked suggestively and Priya gasped. "This stupid thing you did, did it ruin you for marriage?"

"No!" Priya nearly shouted standing up.

Fullerton laughed. "Whoa, calm down there, girl. You have a fiery temper. I just had to ask. But I think I know why you lost whatever job you were trying to get." He laughed again.

Priya felt her face go hot. Was she so easy to read? She needed to be more guarded. More careful. Her impetuousness had gotten her into this situation and was probably going to make her life more difficult if she didn't rein it in.

"Can you help me?" she asked. It was late and she was feeling tired, a little light-headed. She wanted to get this over with and go back home.

"I certainly know a few people who would pay good money for a sweet girl like you," Fullerton said. "Especially one that's still...intact, as they say."

"Pay...?" Priya asked, feeling confused.

"Of course," Fullerton said. "That's why you're here, isn't it? I have a ship leaving in the morning. I don't transport many slaves nowadays. It's technically illegal. But when a girl comes along that will fetch such a high price, well, I can't really say no."

"Slave? What?" Priya mumbled as she stumbled back. She lost her balance and fell to the floor.

"That's it," Fullerton said. "Just let the tea do its work."

"The...tea...?" Priya asked, only just now realizing she had dropped her cup on the carpeted floor. She tried to get up, but she fell to the side as everything went dark.

What had she done?

CHAPTER FIVE

*P*riya awoke when her head hit against something, hard. She winced and tried to raise her hand, but she quickly lost her balance. She forced her eyes open and realized she was laying on the floor of a carriage. She looked up and saw Fullerton staring down at her.

"Drat," he said. "I was hoping you'd be out until we got you onto the ship."

"What ship?" she asked, and then squeezed her eyes shut from the pain. She felt dizzy and nauseous. She tried to reach up to grab the seat across from Fullerton, but only then noticed her hands were bound with ropes. "What's going on?" she demanded.

"I have a shipment of goods sailing out soon bound for the Americas," Fullerton said, looking out the window. "You're going to be on it."

Priya sat up, her senses slowly returning and being replaced by panic. "But...but Indian slavery is illegal!" she said. "The Company outlawed it years ago!"

Fullerton just shrugged. "I've never had a problem finding buyers."

"I'll tell!" Priya said. "I'll tell everyone that Lord Fullerton is a slave trader!"

"No one will listen to you," he said coolly. "Besides, you won't be coming back."

Wouldn't be coming back? Where was she going? How could this happen? She needed to get away. She jumped up and grabbed for the handle of the carriage, but it was locked. Fullerton reached over and pushed her back into the seat.

"Sit down," he ordered. "It's over, girl. Your fate was sealed the moment you knocked on my door."

"The Parkers," Priya said. "They know I went to see you. If I go missing, they will come for you."

"Dumb girl running around Bombay at night," Fullerton said. "Guess you just went missing."

"But the night guards," Priya said. "They saw me. And the butler."

"If I'm not afraid of the British government. Why would I be afraid of them?" Fullerton asked without a hint of malice. It was as though he was just explaining the way of the world to her. "Anything and anyone can be bought for the right price."

And suddenly, Priya was terrified. She knew that this man held all the power, and she had none. Her only hope was to escape when they got to the port. If he managed to get her on that ship, it would all be over.

The port was bustling with activity. There must have been thousands of people from all walks of life coming and going, loading and unloading ships, moving cargo, and hawking their wares. Dozens of ships lined the docks, with their massive masts towering overhead. When the carriage finally came to a stop, Priya's door was opened and a dark hand grabbed her arm and pulled her out. She was shocked to see that it was Fullerton's Indian butler who held her fast.

"Help me!" she said. "Let me go!"

The man's face looked pained, but he shook his head. "You know I cannot."

She looked back at the smug smile on Fullerton's face. She knew that the butler would not risk angering Fullerton and losing his job. She wanted to hate the man for it. For sacrificing one of his own people to please his master. But she knew far too many people who would do the same thing in his position.

She squirmed and twisted, doing her best to pull free from the man's grip so she could get away, but it was no good. He was too strong. Another one of Fullerton's men came around the side of the carriage and grabbed her other arm. Together, they moved her through the crowd of people toward the ships.

"Help me!" she screamed, trying another tact. "I'm being kidnapped! Help me!" Surely, someone in this crowd of people would object to a girl being stolen and sold into slavery. Several people looked her way, but when their eyes fell on Lord Fullerton, casually strolling behind her, they averted their gaze.

Priya was losing hope. How could this happen? How could no one step in?

A loud roar rang out so deafening, everyone stopped for a moment and went silent. Priya looked up and saw a tiger in a cage being hoisted upon a ship. But she wasn't roaring for herself. Back on the dock, three tiger cubs were in a basket and a white man was holding one of them up proudly.

"Get your own tiger!" the man called out. "Raise it from

a babe as your own cat! Or have the fiercest guard dog on the block! Get your own tiger right now!"

The mother tiger roared again, and a few people laughed at her obvious distress. Priya was sickened. These people had no respect for life—human or animal. She thought back to the Evans family and how casually they had disregarded the life of the kitten.

Suddenly, she wondered if in her anger she had caused the Evans family to manifest right before her eyes! She blinked and shook her head. No, she wasn't imagining things. It was the Evans family. Sahib and Memsahib Evans and their son were looking at the tiger cub. Just then, she remembered Sahib Evans's promise to his son. *Don't worry, son. We'll get you another kitten. A better one*, he had said. This was what he must have meant. By better, he meant bigger. Deadlier.

As much as she hated those people, surely, they wouldn't let a girl they knew be dragged away and sold into slavery, would they?

"Sahib Evans!" she called out. "Help me! I'm being kidnapped! Help me!"

Sahib Evans looked down at her. He then looked around, confusion on his face, as if she could have been talking to someone else.

"Help me!" she cried out again.

Sahib Evans then nudged his wife to get her attention. She looked up at him, and he motioned at Priya.

"Help!" she screamed. "Help me! I'm being kidnapped! Help me! Find Sahib Parker!"

Memsahib Evans's face darkened. She did not look concerned for Priya in the slightest. She turned her head away, back to the man selling the tiger cubs, and helped her son pick one out.

Priya was in shock. She couldn't believe what was happening.

Sahib Evans seemed to hesitate. He tapped his wife on the shoulder, but his wife swatted his hand away. She then said something sharp to him. He then followed her lead and turned his back on Priya.

Priya's fear was replaced with rage. How could these people be so cruel? They were perhaps the only people in all of Bombay, in all of India, who could save her, and they chose to do nothing. Tears filled her eyes. Anger, hopelessness, fear. It all came washing over her. There was nothing she could do to keep from being put on that ship and sold into slavery in the Americas.

When they arrived at the gangplank, the ship's captain came down to greet Fullerton.

"What's this?" the captain asked as the men shook hands. "I don't recall seeing any young girls on the manifest."

"A late-night addition," Fullerton said and he dropped a bag of coins into the captain's hand. "I hope it won't be a problem."

The captain shook the bag and then smiled. "Not at all, sir," he said. He motioned for two of his men to take her. Fullerton's men handed her over, and then Fullerton doffed his hat at her and walked away.

As the men continued to drag her up the gangplank, Priya struggled, kicking and screaming to get away or for someone to help her. She knew it was in vain. There were hundreds of people around, all witnesses to this crime, yet no one stepped in to save her. There was no escape. And yet, she fought.

The men forced her down some steep stairs into the ship's hull. They took her past kegs and crates and bags of goods, animal pelts, and live monkeys and parrots, and tossed her into a cage. She scrambled to her feet and ran to the gate as it was closed shut and one of the men locked it with a key.

The man reached his hand through and patted her cheek. "I'm sure I'll be seeing you again later," he said.

Priya didn't even stop to think before spitting at the man. But the man only laughed as he and the other man walked away.

Priya looked around her cell. There were several cages along the wall. She wondered how many other people had been transported to the Americas the same way. At least she seemed to be the only person being transported on this ship. The ban on selling Indians as slaves must have been working for the most part. Fullerton and the captain probably didn't sell slaves often, just when someone was stupid enough to fall right on their doorstep.

Up above, she saw a large hatch pulled open and a crate was lowered down into the hull. It was the cage with the tiger! The men worked to line up the crate with the cage next to Priya. Then they opened the door to the cage and the crate and poked at the tiger with sharp sticks to get her to move into the cage. The tiger lunged and snapped at the men, trying with all her might to kill all of them. Any of them. Priya didn't blame her. She'd gladly help the tiger overthrow their captors if she could. But eventually, the tiger was ushered into the cage, which the men then locked behind her.

"Good job, men," the captain said, slapping them on their backs. "That tiger, she's damn fearless."

The men laughed, congratulating each other on successfully loading the tiger onto the ship. They then worked to remove the crate and finish loading the remainder of the goods. They lowered a palate of hundreds of bags of rice on to the ship. She knew it was rice because rice grains were seeping out of holes in the bags. She wondered for a moment why the captain would be exporting rice. Didn't they have rice overseas?

Priya moved against the wall, looking out of a porthole window to the dock. She could still see countless people moving about, but she didn't bother yelling or waving at them. She knew that no one would help her.

Then, she felt the ship rock to one side, and then the other. She realized that they must have been raising the anchor. She felt her heart freeze and she sank to the floor with her back against the wall, pulling her knees to her chest.

She watched the tiger in the cage next to her. She was pacing, panting. She raised her head and sniffed the air and then let out a strangled cry. She too must have known that the ship was moving.

"Nabhitha," Priya whispered to the tiger, using the Hindi word for fearless. "Those men said you were fearless. But they were wrong. You are just like me. You are terrified."

The tiger was tipped to the right and left, stumbling as she tried to remain upright. She finally gave in and laid down, letting out a sad moan as she did so.

Priya shook her head and placed her head on her knees as she felt the ship pull away from Bombay and out into the open sea.

CHAPTER SIX

*P*riya held her stomach and closed her eyes to keep from vomiting in her cell as the ship rocked back and forth. Nabhitha and the other animals moaned their discomfort as well. Eventually, the ship reached calmer waters away from the busy dock and began floating gently. Priya stood up and looked out her porthole window. She could still see land, though it was some distance away. She wondered if she could swim to shore if she somehow managed to escape her cage.

She walked over to the cage door and shook the bars, but they held fast. She fumbled with the lock, but she had nothing with which to pick it. She heard a low growling and saw that Nabhitha was watching her with interest.

"What do you think?" she asked the tiger. "Can we get out of here?"

Nabhitha let out a snort and Priya laughed. She then realized it was the first time she had laughed in days. And her situation was no laughing matter. She was a captive on a ship sailing to a foreign country where she was going to be sold as a slave. She didn't know much about life as a slave, though she imagined it wouldn't be much different than the way most Indians lived as "servants." But a servant could always quit or be fired. As a servant, she would still have some aspects of freedom and choice. As a slave, she knew she would be in bondage for the rest of her life.

Priya laid her head on the bars of the cage and sighed as she thought of her parents. They must be terrified for her. She never came home last night and now had been gone for most of the day. Would Lucille tell her parents the truth, that she had gone to see Lord Fullerton? Or would she lie and say she never saw her? Priya really had no idea what Lucille would do. But the more she thought about it, she realized that as soon as Lucille figured out something was wrong, she would lie through her teeth to protect herself.

Did Lucille know that Lord Fullerton was a slave trader? Priya shook her head to banish the thought. Surely, in spite of all of their differences, Lucille would never knowingly do something so cruel. So evil. No. Priya couldn't think that of her friend. Besides, Lucille had offered to go with her to see Lord Fullerton in the morning. It was Priya's own impatience that brought her to this place.

Priya grunted in frustration and shook the bars of the cage again. What was she going to do? She had to get out of here! If she waited to escape until after she was in the Americas, she could never get back across the ocean to get home. She needed to escape before the ship lost sight of the Indian coast. But how?

She looked around the ship's hull, hoping to see something that could help her. There were ropes and long sticks that had been whittled into spears. Iron chains and bonds. There were monkeys chained against a wall and a few peafowls running loose. There were crates and crates of goods, some of which were partly open or had holes in them big enough for Priya to figure out what was inside of them. Tiger and leopard skins were in some of them. She saw a basket of rhino horns. A few chairs and tables ornately carved in the Indian style were stacked haphazardly. Rolls of handwoven rugs were piled upon one another. Another crate contained dozens of bronze statues of Hindu gods. And in one crate that was secured very well, she could hear the unmistakable clinking of gold coins as they were knocked about. Some of the other crates she couldn't see into but had a feeling they were full of Britain's prime Indian export: opium.

This was certainly a smugglers ship. Legal and illegal goods extracted from India and the Indian people to be sold to the highest bidder upon the ship's arrival at British colonies in the Americas.

And she was just another thing to be sold.

In spite of the wealth of goods surrounding her, she saw nothing that could help her escape from her cage.

Nabhitha had finally given up on watching Priya and had settled down, laying her head on her massive paws. Massive paws of incredibly sharp claws. Claws that could probably pick a lock with ease if only the tiger knew how.

"Nabhitha," Priya whispered, and the tiger cocked her ears toward her. Priya held the lock to her cage in her hand and the pointed to the similar lock on Nabhitha's door. "You should use your claws to break the locks."

Nabhitha grunted and turned her head away.

Priya crept toward the bars that separated their cages and held out her hand. Maybe she could befriend the tiger and they could work together to escape.

"Hey, come on, girl," Priya said, reaching out as she got down on her haunches and scooted toward the tiger. "We are in this together, right?"

Nabhitha looked back at Priya and let out a low growl. Priya hesitated, but then she smiled and talked in a soothing voice as she reached out to just touch the top of Nabhitha's paw.

"It's okay, girl," Priya said, even though her own hand was shaking and she could feel sweat beading on her forehead. "I'm your friend. We can both escape if we work —Ahh!"

Nabhitha lunged at Priya, ripping at her arm with her claws. Priya screamed as she pulled away and fell back against the far wall of her cell. Nabhitha let out a terrifying roar as she pushed her face against the bars of her cell as though desperately trying to get at Priya to tear her to shreds.

Priya cried in fear and pain. She was almost afraid to look down at her arm, scared that it might be completely gone. By the gods, how could she be so stupid! She felt warm liquid pooling on her skin and knew that her arm must still be there. She finally looked down and saw blood seeping out of three large gashes. She removed the sari wrap from her shoulder and used it to wipe the blood away. She sighed in relief when she realized that the wounds were not deep. Thankfully, the claws had not even ripped into the muscles. The scratches were only flesh wounds.

But did they ever hurt! And she had nothing with which to clean them with. She didn't even have any drinking water. She wiped the blood away and then wrapped her arm with the cloth to stop the bleeding.

Tears fell from her eyes from the pain, her stupidity, and the hopelessness of her situation.

"I'm sorry," she finally said to Nabhitha when she was able to speak. She knew that she should not have tried to touch a tiger. Respect for tigers was something instilled in

Indian youths from infancy. Tigers were usually solitary creatures who avoided humans at all costs. But it was not uncommon to end up in the path of a tiger at some point in a person's life if they spent any time outside of their village. Priya had been raised in the city of Bombay, so there was almost no chance of seeing a tiger there. But she had family in a village a few miles away. Every time she went to visit the village, her mother drilled into her head the importance of showing respect to a tiger should she happen to see one.

"Keep your head down," Amma had said. "Never look the tiger in the eye. Never turn your back."

The key to avoid being eaten by a tiger was to show it the ultimate respect. One must always be humble when in that path of a hungry tiger.

Priya had forgotten that. She had thought for a moment that she and the tiger were equals, or that the tiger was even less than her. A pet. A mere cat. And it could have cost Priya her life.

"Never again," Priya promised Nabhitha. "Never again will I make the mistake of thinking I am above you."

She thought about the Evans family, who had been foolish enough to buy one of Nabhitha's cubs. It was actually fairly common for British families to buy wild animals —even deadly ones—and try to keep them as pets. The situation always ended in tragedy, usually the animal or a human dead—if not both. The lucky animals were released into the wild after they grew too big to control. But since they did not know how to live in the wild, they were usually captured and killed within a few days, if they didn't simply die of starvation.

For a moment, she imagined Nabhitha's kitten getting big enough to attack the boy who dropped the kitten in the well, then she shuddered. No. As much as she hated the

Evans and their bratty child, she could never wish some-thing so awful on a child. She only wished there was something she could do to get the tiger cub back. Reunite the cub with its mother.

She looked over at Nabhitha as she settled back on the floor and licked her paw clean. Even though Nabhitha had just tried to kill her, her heart broke for the mother who had just lost everything. Nabhitha was not her equal, but she was not her enemy. For better or worse, they were in this together.

*t some point, Priya must have fallen asleep, rocked by the gentle motion of the ship on the sea. The sound of the lock on her cage clicking woke her. She opened her eyes and saw the dark figure of a man standing at the door to her cell.

"What?" she mumbled. "Who's there?"

"I told you I'd be seeing you again," said the man with a laugh.

Immediately, Priya was wide awake. She scrambled to her feet and stood with her back flat against the far wall.

"Stay back!" she said, but the man only laughed.

"Or what?" he asked as he stepped into the cell.

"I'll scream," she said. "The captain will hear me and punish you!"

The man laughed again and took another step toward her as he undid the belt on his trousers. "Everyone is at supper," he said. "We have all the time in the world."

She screamed anyway as the man lunged toward her. The animals all sensed her distress and launched into a cacophony of screeches and squawks. He grabbed her shoulders and she raised her arms to block him but immediately felt a surge of pain through her body from her injured arm. Tears flew to her eyes and she could not stop them.

The man hesitated for a moment as he looked at his hand, which was now covered in blood from her injured arm.

"What the hell?" he asked.

Priya darted away from him toward the door to the cell, but he recovered from the surprise quickly. He grabbed her by the hair and pulled her back. She yelped in pain as she fell back into him. She turned and pushed him away and heard him smack into the bars of her cell. She heard him laugh.

Then she heard a scream so chilling it froze the blood in her veins.

Nabhitha roared as she grabbed the man's back. Priya stumbled back in horror. The man turned around and Priya nearly vomited at the sight of the man's back shredded like paper, blood pouring from his ripped flesh. The man screamed again as Nabhitha reached through the bars of her cage and grabbed the man's chest and arm and tried to pull him into her cage. She couldn't bring his whole body through, so she contented herself with his arm, which she brought to her mouth. Her jaw crunched on the man's bones and her teeth tore into the flesh.

The man continued to scream while Priya wept and Nabhitha roared.

CHAPTER SEVEN

The man was still struggling, crying, screaming when Priya heard footsteps on the stairs. She struggled to her feet as several other sailors and the captain came upon the scene.

"My God!" the captain yelled. The men froze, unsure of what to do as Nabhitha hunched over her prey.

The captain looked from the man to Priya. When he saw her bloodied arm and tear-stained face, he nodded with a look of understanding of the situation.

"Well, come on, you fools!" the captain barked. "Get him away from there!"

The men moved into Priya's cell and pulled on the man's legs, but he screamed in pain as Nabhitha dug her claws in further, growling at the men who would dare take her dinner from her.

"Hey! Hey! Hey!" one of the other men yelled from the other side of Nabhitha's cage as he banged on the bars with a stick, trying to get her attention. But still, Nabhitha would not let go of the man.

"Give that to me!" the captain said, taking the sharpened stick away from the sailor. He then stuck the stick into Nabhitha's cage and poked her with it. "Let go, damned beast!" But Nabhitha would not relent. In exasperation, the captain stabbed Nabhitha's paw with the shiv. Nabhitha shrieked, but she let go of the man and moved to the opposite side of the cage to nurse her wound.

The sailors then dragged the man out of Priya's cell, leaving a trail of blood behind him.

The men gathered around him so Priya could no longer see his mangled body.

"He's dead, sir," one of the men said.

The sailors let out mumbled curses and gasps.

"But...but he...he was screaming..." Priya mumbled, feeling sick.

"Must have been the shock. And the blood loss," the captain said, shaking his head as he looked at the mess of blood on the floor. "Toss him overboard."

"W-w-what?" one of the men asked. "Are...are you sure, captain? Shouldn't we take him back to land? Give him a decent burial?"

The captain pointed at Priya. "What do you think he was doing in the cage in the first place?"

The men looked Priya, but then quickly turned away shamefaced.

"This man died a dishonorable death," the captain said. "And he'll be given a dishonorable burial."

"Aye-aye, captain," the men said as two of them struggled to drag the man away.

"You two there," the captain said to two other sailors. "Clean this mess up. And *mind* the tiger!"

"Yes, sir," one of them said.

"But, sir," the other man said. "Shouldn't we dispatch

the tiger as well? She's dangerous. Got the taste for blood now."

"That tiger is worth more than the whole lot of you put together!" the captain said harshly. "Her buyer only wants her for sport anyway. The fiercer, the better."

"Yes, sir," the men said as they worked to gather buckets and mops to clean the mess.

The captain then turned to Priya and motioned for her to follow him. Priya hesitated. It was as though her feet were nailed to their spot on the floor. She was surrounded by danger and couldn't trust anyone.

The captain sighed in annoyance. "Ain't no harm going to come to you, gal," he said. "You're worth a pretty penny yourself. That man got what was coming to him."

Priya gulped and then forced her feet to move toward the door of her cell. She did her best to step around the pools of blood, but she was horrified to see her own bloody footprints following her toward the stairs. She took one last look at Nabhitha, who was still crouched in the back of her cell licking her wound, before gripping the steep stairs and crawling out of the hull.

Priya had been captured for less than a day, so she was surprised at the sense of relief that washed over her as she breathed in the fresh sea air. She hadn't had time to notice how stifling it was below deck. It was early evening, so it was still light out even though the sun was setting quickly. She took in a deep breath, thankful to still be alive and relatively unharmed after all she had been through.

"Easy! Easy!" she heard one of the men yell. She looked over just as some of the men were tossing her attacker's body over the side of the ship. She quickly looked away, but still heard the unceremonious splash as his body hit the water.

"Come here, girl," the captain said, motioning for her to follow him to the ship's edge. "Give me your arm."

She raised her arm, with more than a little wincing, and she sucked in a breath as he unwrapped the cloth.

The captain whistled when he saw the slashes on her arm. "Nasty cuts," he said. "But you'll live." He picked up a bucket and ordered her to hold her arm over the edge of the ship. "This is going to hurt like hell," he warned.

Priya screamed as he poured salty seawater over her wounds.

"I know it burns," the captain said. "But it will keep the wounds from getting infected. The last thing either of us is going to want is to have to chop off that arm from gangrene."

Priya whimpered at the thought and the captain chuckled. He pulled out a fresh bandage roll and wrapped her arm tightly.

"Don't worry," he said. "I've taken care of more than my fair share of battle wounds. This will heal nicely. You'll have a hell of a scar, but it will make for a great story one day. The girl with tiger stripes."

Priya nodded and ran her hand over the bandage, surprised that the scratches already hurt less than they did a few minutes ago. Politeness prodded at her to thank the captain for helping her, but she fought the urge. After all, he was still a bad man. A smuggler. A slave trader. By taking care of her, he was only taking care of his "investment."

The captain seemed to sense her reticence to trust him. "You must be starving," he said. "Why don't you follow me to my quarters."

She was starving. And thirsty. And tired. She wondered if the blood loss she had sustained was also having an effect on her because she was feeling more than a little nauseous.

She didn't want to trust the captain, but she believed he intended to keep her unviolated—at least for now—so he could get a higher price for her at the slave market later. So, she followed him.

His quarters were nicer than any she could have imagined existing on a ship. It was as though she had slipped into Memsahib Parker's bedroom. There was a large four-poster bed in one corner with plenty of blankets and pillows. There was also a desk as lovely as the one that had been in Lord Fullerton's office. There were books and statues and various other trinkets strewn about.

But at the smell of freshly baked bread and roasted vegetables, her mouth began to water uncontrollably. She practically had to wipe the drool from her mouth as a servant sailor placed two plates of food on a dining table and then left the room.

"Please," the captain said, indicating she should take a seat by one of the plates of food.

She wanted to walk over slowly, show some dignity, but she was famished and completely parched. She rushed to the table and drank a full tankard of water before ripping into the bread.

The captain chuckled as he refilled her cup. "Slow down," he said, "before you choke. And take a seat."

Priya did as she was ordered, taking her seat and picking up the silverware to eat more properly. When she finally ate enough to feel her belly filling, she spoke.

"What's to become of me?" she asked.

The captain took a swig of ale from his own cup. "First, a very long journey," he said. "Do you know where Jamaica is?"

She shrugged. "America," she said.

"An island off of Central America," the captain clarified,

though it didn't make much difference to her. "Largest slave market in the world is there."

"So, I am to be sold," she said, the food turning sour in her stomach.

"Aye," the captain said. "But not on the block like a common negro. You are Indian, young, not...unpleasant to look at. A private auction will be held for you among the elite buyers. You'll fetch a high price for a good placement."

She snorted. As if there was such a thing as a "good" placement for a slave.

"You know what I mean," the captain said.

"I'm afraid I don't," Priya said.

"You know, placement in a rich home as a house slave. Probably a lady's maid," he clarified.

Priya nodded. The British women in India often had personal lady's maids. And while they were usually well-fed and well-dressed, they also bore the brunt of their memsahib's ill-treatment. And not a few were the victims of attention by the sahib as well. Priya thought she'd rather toil in the fields of some large plantation. It would be hard work but at least she'd be alone.

But she knew he had no choice in the matter.

"It will take us about one to two months to get there, depending on the wind," the captain went on, and Priya nearly spit her drink.

"One to two months?" she exclaimed.

"We will stop in Goa first," the captain explained. "Pick up the last of our goods. Then we sail for England. We will make a quick stop there, unload some of this stuff. Then we head to Jamaica to auction off the rest."

Priya rubbed her forehead. She had no idea how far away that all was, but it sounded like a world and lifetime away. By the time she reached Jamaica, her parents would surely think she was dead. And she didn't imagine she would ever find her way home again. How could she? It would be impossible.

"Of course," the captain said, standing and walking around the table to her. "It would be a shame for you to have to spend the entire journey in that cage."

Priya started. She wasn't concerned about that in the slightest. She knew she would have to spend the whole of the trip in her cell next to Nabhitha. The captain placed his hand on hers and held it fast. Priya's heart beat fast as she tried to tug it away.

"I could arrange...*other* quarters for you, if you'd like," he went on, leaning toward her. "My quarters, you understand."

"No!" Priya said, standing up but being unable to move away as long as he held her hand in his. "I don't understand. That...that man. The one the tiger killed. You said he was dishonorable!"

"Indeed, he was!" the man said. "On this ship, you belong to me. And no other man shall touch you. And I know you will bring a lot more at auction if I can vouch for your...purity."

"But I won't be pure if you take me," Priya said, still struggling to release her hand from his grasp.

"I won't take you, I promise you that," the captain said. "But there are other things you could do for me." He reached up with his other hand and cupped her cheek, running this thumb across her lips. "Other ways you could keep me company on the long, long journey ahead. And you could stay here, in lavish comfort, all the food and drink you could wish. A veritable pleasure cruise, wouldn't you agree?"

"No!" Priya shouted again, slapping his hand away. "I'd

never debase myself with a horrid man like you! You disgust me! You're no better than the man the tiger killed! I wish she were here right now!"

The captain laughed. "You think that stupid tiger was protecting you? She just saw an easy dinner." He grabbed her injured arm and held it up, causing her to gasp in pain. "She'd just as sooner gobble you up, you ungrateful slut."

"Stop!" she cried. "Please, let me go!"

The captain let out a grunt and released her, then pushed her to the floor. "We will see how long you last below deck," he sneered. "A few days down there in that stinking hull and you'll be begging to share my bed."

Priya scrambled to her feet and ran toward the door.

"Here," the captain said. She looked and saw he was holding out a basket toward her. "Food, water, clothes. You won't live in luxury down there, but I won't have you showing up at port looking like a scrawny rat. Robust girls bring the most cash."

She hesitated, but then took a few cautious steps back toward him. She reached out to take the basket, but he was holding it tightly.

"Say thank you," he grumbled.

She pressed her lips tight. She did not want to be beholden to this disgusting man in any way. But she knew that her very survival depended on him for now. If she angered him too greatly, he could kill her in an instant. He might want the large payout he would receive for selling her, but his whole ship was laden with expensive, illicit goods. If he lost her, it would be no great thing in the long run.

"Thank you," she mumbled.

The captain placed his hand to his ear. "What was that?" he asked. "I couldn't quite hear you."

"Thank you!" she said, loudly and clearly.

"That's more like it," the captain said, releasing the basket. "I'll teach you a few manners yet."

Priya took the basket and headed toward the door. *Not if I teach you first*, she thought.

CHAPTER EIGHT

The captain did not accompany Priya back to her cell himself, but sent one of the other sailors with her to make sure she was locked back inside securely. Nabhitha let out a low growl at the sailor as he passed her cage, which sent him quickly scurrying back up the stairs to the main deck, but she quieted back down as soon as he was out of sight and went back to nursing her wounded paw.

"Did the captain hurt you very badly?" Priya asked. Nabhitha let out what sounded like a low whine, but she didn't stop licking. Priya was actually a little surprised that the captain had taken a stab at Nabhitha, considering her incredible value. But she supposed people often reacted without thinking when faced with a man-eating tiger.

Priya went through her basket and found a pillow and blanket, a couple of simple saris, a water skein, and some fruit, vegetables, fresh bread, and meat. She wasn't hungry at the moment, since she had eaten at the captain's table, so she put the food aside for the time being and placed the pillow and blanket on the cell's "bed," which was a wooden frame with some ropes tied across it to form a mattress. She shook her head. The next few weeks were going to be uncomfortable indeed.

She looked around and saw a bucket in one corner. It took her a moment to realize that the bucket was her toilet. She nearly retched at the thought. She then realized she did not have enough water to wash her body, much less her hair. He looked out the porthole and saw only blackness, as the sun had completely set. She couldn't see any lights from the shore, if they were even within sight of it, or any stars from this angle. There was at least light inside the hull due to some haphazardly hung about lanterns.

Priya sunk down on her bed with her back against the wall. She pulled her knees up to her chest and began to cry. She had always thought that life as a servant was not much better than life as a slave. She now knew she had been very wrong. Life could always get much, much worse. She had always wondered why her parents seemed contented—and sometimes grateful—for the life they had with the Parkers. Sure, they had food, clothes, and a roof over their heads, but they had very little more than that, especially when compared with the British families. She wondered if somehow her parents knew just how bad life could be without the protection of the Parkers. Of course, it could also be much better. If the British had not come to India, then at least the people in charge would be other Indians. She had no way of knowing if that would have made her life better or not, but she didn't think it could be much worse. She had lived a fairly good life. She had even been able to go to school. But there were not that many British families in India. Working for a family was a craved position. Most other Indians worked in factories, mines, or on plantations. She wondered if her parents were content because they knew life could be worse. They might have dreamed of a better life, but a worse one was a very real possibility. Is this what they were afraid of when Priya lost her chance at a position with another family? She supposed her parents were lucky that they were not fired as well. What would they have done without their positions with the Parkers? Where would they have gone? What would have happened to Priya?

She probably would have ended up in a place like this. A poorly paid worker routinely abused at the hands of a cruel taskmaster.

But at least she would still be with her parents. They would have each other.

Priya had messed up. And she didn't see a way out to correct her mistakes. There was no way to escape. At least not for now. She would have to keep her eyes open for opportunities to get off this ship and get home. The captain had said they were going to stop in Goa first. Goa was a large city south of Bombay. She could surely find her way home from there. It would be her last—and probably only —way to escape before the ship headed out into open waters and England. If she ended up in England, any chance of getting home would probably be lost to her. She had to escape in Goa.

She heard Nabhitha make a panting, whimpering sound. She looked over and saw that the tiger was breathing rapidly. She appeared to be in some sort of distress.

"Hey," Priya said, climbing off her bed and inching toward Nabhitha's cage on her knees. "Hey, Nabhitha. It's okay. What's wrong, girl?"

Nabhitha tried to stand, but she moaned when she put weight on her foot. She inched closer to the side of the cage she shared with Priya, but Priya stayed well away from the tiger's reach.

"I'm sorry, girl," Priya said. "I know your paw must hurt, but I don't have anything that can help you."

Nabhitha moaned again and then laid down, leaning up against the bars of the cage. Even though Priya knew that Nabhitha was a dangerous animal, her heart ached for her. She was scared, missed her babies, and was in pain. Priya got up and shook the bars of her cage.

"Hello!" she yelled. "Hey! I need help!"

The sailor who had taken her back to her cage earlier came rushing down the stairs. "What's wrong?" he asked as though in a panic. He let out a sigh of relief when he saw Priya. "I thought maybe the old girl had ripped you up." He motioned toward the tiger.

"She's hurt," Priya said. "Badly. We need to clean her wound. And she needs food and water."

"I'm not getting anywhere near that thing," the sailor said. "Jacob was my good mate. Do you hear me?"

Priya assumed Jacob was the man Nabhitha had eaten, the one who had tried to rape her.

Priya gripped the bars of her cage. "Jacob had it coming," she growled through gritted teeth. "But this tiger is valuable. Worth more than that piece of scum ever was. You better tell the captain that the tiger needs attention before he tosses *you* overboard."

The sailor's face went pale and he scuttled up the stairs like a crab. Priya sighed, hoping her threats came to something. Honestly, she didn't know how anyone could help Nabhitha. If anyone got too close, Nabhitha would surely cause them great injury. The scratches on her arm were proof enough of that.

The sailor came back down the stairs with a small crate, which he placed in front of Priya's cell.

"The captain says that since the tiger killed Jacob defending you, it's your job to keep her alive," the sailor said.

"What?" Priya asked, nearly laughing. "Is he joking?"

"I don't think so, miss," he said. "He said the both of you were already causing him too much trouble, and he wouldn't miss the pair of ya."

Priya was angry, but not entirely surprised. She guessed that the captain would spend the next four weeks looking for any way to make her life harder until she agreed to be his sex slave, which she would never do. She'd rather die.

"Then give the supplies to me, you coward!" she spat. She reached through the bars to the crate but yelped when the sailor grabbed her injured arm and squeezed.

"Watch yourself, missy," the man said, his eyes glaring at her. Priya stared back at him with equal fierceness. "I won't miss a chance to get revenge for my friend."

"Does it make you feel brave to threaten an injured girl in a cage?" she asked him. "Because I think it just makes you look like even more of a coward."

The sailor snorted and shook her arm as he released his grip. He stood up and stomped over to the side of the room and grabbed a barrel, which he rolled over next to her cage. He took the top off, revealing that it was full of water. Priya realized that it must have been more of the supplies the captain ordered the sailor to give her. Then the man went back to the stairs.

"I hope that tiger rips your face off," the man yelled at

her over his shoulder. "And ain't none of us going to come to your aid."

"I wouldn't expect you to," Priya shouted as he bounded up the stairs. Priya sighed in relief. Even though she had spoken boldly, she had been terrified of what the man could do to her. But now that he was gone, she had a new fear —Nabhitha.

Nabhitha was still lying by the bars of the cage. Her breathing had slowed, but it still seemed labored.

Priya opened the crate and pulled out the goods the captain had sent. A bottle of some sort of clear alcohol was there, some bandages, and several hunks of fresh meat. She felt a little sick as she remembered seeing Jacob's flailed back, his flesh falling from his bones. But then she forced herself to remember that this meat wasn't Jacob. She had seen the men throw him overboard.

Priya picked up one of the meat chunks and walked over to Nabhitha. "Here, girl," she said, and tossed it toward her. It landed inside Priya's cage, but within claw's length of Nabhitha. Nabhitha's ears perked up and she stuck out her tongue toward the meat, but she made no move to grab it. She seemed to want it, but too lethargic to make a move to eat it.

Priya inched closer and nudged the meat toward Nabhitha with her foot. Nabhitha lazily opened her eyes and watched the meat and Priya, but she didn't open her mouth to eat it until the meat was right in front of her face. Even then, she didn't snap at it—or Priya—but ate the meat gently. Priya wondered if Nabhitha was growing used to her presence.

When Nabhitha finished the meat, she gave Priya a longing look. Priya pressed her lips into a thin line and then reached into the crate for the next chunk of meat. This time she stepped closer to the cage bars and dropped the meat right in front of Nabhitha's face. Nabhitha didn't so much as growl as she ate the meat.

Priya knew it was probably foolish, but she felt like she and Nabhitha had a rapport going. A rapport she would need if she hoped to get close enough to Nabhitha's paw to pour the alcohol on it.

For the final hunk of meat, Priya walked right up to the cage and held it over Nabhitha's face. Nabhitha sniffed the meat and then opened her mouth, allowing Priya to feed it to her. Priya smiled and almost laughed. She was feeding a tiger! In all her life she had never experienced something so incredible. Tigers were an object of fascination and of respect, but mostly of fear.

When Nabhitha was finished eating, she laid her head back down and closed her eyes. Priya held her breath and took a chance. She reached her hand through the cage and placed it on Nabhitha's head.

Nabhitha didn't move.

Priya slowly moved her hand back and forth between Nabhitha's ears, petting the softest fur she had ever touched.

Nabhitha let out a small growl, which Priya took as a warning that Nabhitha was done being petted like a common house cat, and she backed off. She sat on her haunches and watched Nabhitha, wondering if it was wise to try and treat Nabhitha's paw. She thought it was rather poor form of her to use this newfound comradery to cause Nabhitha more pain. But if she waited too long to treat Nabhitha's wound, Nabhitha could sicken and die.

Priya pulled out the bottle of alcohol and the bandages. She unwrapped her arm and called out to get Nabhitha's attention. Nabhitha opened her eyes and watched as Priya poured the alcohol over her own wounds. Priya winced in pain, but she gritted her teeth to bear it.

"See, Nabhitha," Priya said. "It hurts, but it is for the best. It will keep you from getting sick." She then wrapped her arm back in the bandages. "Now, you."

Nabhitha grunted and wrinkled her nose a bit, but she didn't budge. Her paw was still laying very near the bars of the cage. Priya inched closer, Nabhitha's ever watchful eyes on her.

"I'm just going to pour the alcohol over your injury, okay?" Priya explained to the tiger. The tiger let out a little grunt, but she didn't move. Priya sat on her heels, ready to launch herself as far away from Nabhitha as possible at the first hint of aggression.

Priya reached out, slowly tipping the jar over Nabhitha's paw. The alcohol flowed out and splashed on Nabhitha's wound. Nabhitha sat up quickly and let out a roar. Priya jumped back.

"I'm sorry!" Priya said. "But it is necessary if you want to live!"

Nabhitha let out another, smaller growl and backed away from the cage bars. She went to the other side of the room and curled up into a ball.

Priya waited for her heart to return to its normal place in her chest before she dared to move again. She then put the lid back on the alcohol and put it with her other things, along with the unused bandages. She took a drink of water from the barrel and poured some of the water into a small bucket for Nabhitha, which she put near the bars of the cage where Nabhitha's tongue could reach it if she wanted it. All the while, Nabhitha's eyes watched her from across the room.

Priya then laid down on her bed and tried to get some

sleep. She was glad she had been able to treat Nabhitha's wound, but she wondered just how much damage she had done to their relationship in the process. Would Nabhitha ever trust her again? As she drifted off to sleep, a smile crossed her face. She realized that when she poured the alcohol on Nabhitha's foot that even though Nabhitha was in terrible pain, she never took a swipe at her.

CHAPTER NINE

Over the next few days, as the ship meandered up the coast, Nabhitha's health seemed to improve. She didn't lick her wound as much and her energy levels returned. Every day, the sailor brought a fresh supply of meat for Nabhitha and some food for Priya. And every morning he seemed disappointed to find both of them still alive. Priya would just smirk as she took the food from him, and he would stomp his way back to the top deck.

Priya continued feeding Nabhitha by hand each day, and they both seemed to grow more comfortable in each other's company. Though, Priya never let herself forget that Nabhitha was wild and could turn on her at any time. She unwrapped her arm, and was both proud and disappointed at the scars that were forming as the wounds healed. She was proud she had escaped the tiger's grip and had learned a valuable lesson, but she was sad her body had been permanently marked by the experience. She just shrugged and chalked it up to one more thing she would have to learn to accept in this life.

Much like accepting her life as a slave if she didn't find a way off this ship. As the ship neared Goa, she became more and more anxious. Restless. She hadn't come up with any sort of plan to get out of her cell, off the ship, and into Goa once they arrived. She had no weapons or tools and no allies who could help her. She wondered if she shouldn't try to seduce the sailor who was in charge of watching her so he would open the door to her cage, but she decided that was too risky. He should be able to easily see through her rouse. And if he didn't, what would she do once he entered her cell? How would she fight him off? And if she did, how would she then avoid the dozens of other sailors and get off the ship? She racked and racked her brain but could not come up with any sort of realistic plan to escape. All she could do was pray that an opportunity would present itself while they were docked in Goa.

She had never been overly religious. She went through the motions of prayers and fasting and visits to the temple and was respectful of her parents' views, but she knew she had never taken it to heart or really put much faith in the gods.

Her mother had been pestering her to connect with a god or goddess of her own in recent years, to find her isht-devta, the god or goddess who would eventually lead her soul to salvation. "Who will watch you and protect you once you leave my house?" her mother had asked. At the time, Priya had only shrugged and not given it much thought. She never really imagined she would be far from her mother's guidance and protection. Family was everything to Indians. Even if Priya married and had children of her own, she would always return to her mother for comfort and support.

But now her mother could not be further away from her. She should have listened. A personal goddess would be a great comfort to her right now. She wondered if after a lifetime of ignoring them if the gods would hear her now.

Priya felt the ship's movements slow and then a sharp tug to the left and a large splash. She jumped up and looked out the window. In the distance, she could see a very busy port lined with dozens of ships. The ship she was on didn't pull up to any of the docks, but remained anchored out at sea. The captain must have been planning to travel to and from the city by longboat. Priya cursed to herself. This made any chance of escape even more unlikely. If she could get out of her cage and up on deck, how would she get to shore? She couldn't row a boat by herself. And she wasn't a very good swimmer. Sure, she had spent many summers playing in rivers and streams with her cousins and friends, but actual swimming in water any more than waist-deep was rare.

She was feeling despair wash over her when she saw a small boat heading for the ship. Soldiers! They must have been customs officials heading out to inspect the boat! She was saved! If the British loved anything, is was money. And they couldn't tax illegal goods. Once they saw all this illegal stuff on the ship, surely the officials would do something. And the slave trade was certainly illegal! Once they saw her, they would surely demand she be freed! She was saved. She reached her arm through the porthole and waved, screaming for help at the officials. They didn't seem to hear her, though, as they never looked her way as the little boat passed by. No matter. They would have to board the ship and then come below deck to inspect the goods. She would make sure they saw her then.

Priya paced the cage excitedly. Nabhitha seemed to take notice of this and watched her with interest.

"We are going to get out of here," Priya said. "Don't

worry. I won't leave you behind. I'll make sure they take you to shore too and set you free."

Nabhitha seemed to like this idea, as she promptly sat by the door of her cage and waited to see what would happen.

Priya could hear the busy footsteps of the sailors on the upper deck as they ran about doing...whatever it was that sailors did. Priya had never been on a ship before so she had no idea what it took to operate one. But soon it wouldn't be her concern any longer because she would be free of this prison.

Finally, she heard the sounds she had been waiting for. The voices of three men carried down the stairs, along with the clomping of their boots. Priya pressed herself up so hard against the bars she almost thought she could melt through them. Her heart soared as the captain appeared with two customs officials—and one of them was Indian!

Indian men were allowed to serve in the British army, but they were usually allowed to only ever be militiamen. Infantry. Very few were ever allowed to move up in ranks or hold any higher positions. The fact that this man—who looked to be no more than twenty—held a customs position spoke very well of him indeed! He would surely speak up and make sure she was released.

"I'm sure you men will see that everything down here is on the up and up," the captain said.

"Except for the slave you are transporting!" Priya called out as she shook the bars of the cage.

The Indian man saw her and his eyes went white and his skin blanched. He looked almost as though he was going to be sick. The other man, however, the British man, paid her no mind at all. He looked right past her and over her head. Anywhere but directly at her, as though she wasn't even there.

"Right," the British customs official said. "What's in this box here?" He moved over to a stack of crates by one wall.

"Only the finest of British exports, sir," the captain said.

"I'll need to take a sample of that back for...further examination," the customs officer said.

"Of course, sir," the captain said.

"Hey!" Priya called out. "Hey! Please, let me out! I've been kidnapped! He's going to sell me as a slave. Help me!"

But all three of them continued to ignore her! Even the Indian officer looked away, though he did pull at his collar as though it was choking him.

Priya couldn't believe it. How could they just ignore what was happening to her?

"These silks are the finest in all of India. Handwoven," the captain said. "I'm sure your wife would appreciate the vibrancy of the dye."

The customs official nodded. "I'll need five bolts of that as well. And, let's not beat around the bush, captain. I'll need at least five hundred pounds in order to issue the clearance papers."

By the gods! Priya realized what was happening. The customs official was extracting a bribe in order to look away! He didn't care what the captain was smuggling as long as he got his cut.

"You can't do this!" Priya yelled. "I need help! I need to get home!"

"Sir," the Indian official finally whispered to his commander. "Perhaps...there is something..."

"What?" the British official asked loudly. "Do you dare to say something to me? I told you when you were assigned to me that you were to shut your mouth and do what you're told. Did I not make myself clear?"

"O...of course, sir," the man said. "I just...I just thought..."

"You thought nothing," the British man sneered. "You are not here to think. You're here to work. Take these goods back to the boat and cover them with a tarp, now!"

"Yes, sir," the Indian man said, properly cowed. He rushed over and grabbed the items that were to be paid for the bribe and started taking them upstairs. But as he did so, he gave Priya a pitiful look of apology.

Priya gave him a nod of understanding. There was nothing he could do. He reminded Priya of her parents. If he valued his position, he would say nothing, even at the cost of his fellow Indians. Self-preservation seemed to be the name of the game.

"My parents are Vivaan and Charvi," Priya called out to him. "They work for Sahib Parker in Bombay. Please tell them I am alive!"

"Shut your damn mouth," the captain said as he stomped over toward her. But Nabhitha jumped up on the bars of her cage and growled, causing him to stumble back.

"Why are you dawdling?" the British customs official snapped at the Indian man. "Get moving!"

"Tell them!" Priya yelled as the Indian man stumbled up the stairs. "Tell them I will come back! I will find a way to come back!"

As soon as the customs officials were out of sight, the captain reached through the bars of Priya's cage and grabbed her sari, pulling her close to him.

"I bet you thought that was real smart, didn't you?" the captain growled into her face so close she could feel the heat of his breath on her cheek.

Nabhitha, in her own cage, crouched down and bared her teeth as if she was about to strike. But they all knew she couldn't attack anyone, which only seemed to frustrate her further as her tail swished from side to side.

"When are you going to learn, girl," the captain continued, "that I *own* you! You are never going to get out of here unless it is in chains at the auction house."

At that, the captain released his grip on her sari and she stepped away. As the captain left, Nabhitha once again jumped up on the bars of her cage, growling and swiping her paws at him.

The captain only laughed at her as he reached the stairs. "You girls can spit and strike all you want. It won't change anything."

After the captain was gone, Priya ran back to her porthole window and watched for the customs officials' boat. A few minutes later, she saw it. The British officer was facing the dock and the Indian official was facing the ship. The British official seemed to be still berating the young man.

Priya stuck her arm through the porthole and waved. This time, the Indian official looked up at her. He pressed his lips together grimly, but then she was sure she saw him give a small nod. She sighed in relief. She knew he would contact her parents. It was a small victory. Too small. But it was at least more than she had before.

CHAPTER TEN

*a*fter the customs officials left, Priya expected the ship to depart, but it did not. Instead, she watched as the longboats shuttled sailors from the ship to the city at least half a dozen times as evening approached. She figured the sailors must be going into Goa to enjoy one last night of debauchery before heading out to sea for the next several weeks. Even if she had managed to get out of her cage and to the upper deck, she never would have been able to avoid so many men. Even now, after so many had been taken to shore, she could hear the heavy footsteps of the men left behind to guard the ship and its valuable cargo.

She sat on her bed, unsure of what she should be doing or feeling. Of course, there was nothing she could actually do, but she felt restless. Useless. As though she should be doing *something*. She had never been so idle.

She wavered between feeling despondent and angry. Sad seemed to be the logical feeling at the moment. She was trapped on a smuggler's ship with no chance of escape. She was going to be sold as a slave thousands of miles from home. She would never see her parents or her homeland again. She should feel like giving up.

But anger burned in the bottom of her belly. How could humans treat each other like this? Like chattel. The British and the Americans had been treating Africans and Indians this way for centuries. Indian slavery was outlawed now, but it had only been illegal for a few years. And the way many Indians were treated today was similar to being slaves. The British sometimes even enslaved their own people—only they called it "indentured servitude." The British were experts at giving polite names to impolite situations. What was it the ladies often said when they needed to use the chamber pot? "I think I'll take a walk in the garden," was what Memsahib Parker usually said.

Thinking of Memsahib Parker reminded her of the Evans family, and how they turned their backs on her at the port in Bombay. Such dreadful, cruel people! For as long as she lived, she would never forget that. If only there were some way, any way she could get revenge for that. But since she doubted she would ever return to India, she didn't imagine she would ever see the Evans family again. But maybe she would. She was on her way to the New World to be sold as a slave. Who knew where she would end up. She might be sold to a British family who would one day take her to England. All British families in India eventually went back home. If she ended up in England, one day the Evans family would be there too. She had to have faith that one day, she and the Evans family would face each other again. It gave her something to look forward to.

"I don't know what is going to happen to either of us when we get to Jamaica, Nabhitha," Priya said as she picked up a chunk of meat and handed it to Nabhitha through the shared bars of their cages. "But I'll never abandon you or forget you, or your babies. I don't know what happened to all of your cubs, but I know which family took one of them. If I ever get back to India, or just end up in England, wherever I am when I see the Evans family again, I promise to avenge all of us."

Nabhitha took the meat and then made a sort of rolling, breathy noise, a chuffing that sounded almost like a purr. Priya took that as a sign of approval. Nabhitha then put her nose and mouth through the bars of her cage and looked at Priya. Priya did not see any anger or aggression in Nabhitha's face. She slowly reached up and placed her shaking hand on Nabhitha's nose. Nabhitha pulled her head back and licked the palm of Priya's hand. Priya exhaled and rubbed the side of Nabhitha's face, her fingers getting lost in the thick fur.

Priya gave thanks to the gods that Nabhitha had honored her with her friendship. She had been too hasty before. She could not make friends with a tiger—the tiger had to decide that Priya was worthy of her friendship.

"You and me, Nabhitha," Priya whispered. "You and me until the end."

The next morning, the ship raised anchor early in the morning. Priya listened as the sailors rushed about, whistles blew, and the captain barked orders. As the sun rose, the ship pulled away from Goa and out into the open sea. Priya watched with a heavy heart as the Indian coastline grew smaller and smaller until she could not see it at all. Then she felt nauseous as the ship tossed about on the rolling sea. But finally, the sea calmed, as did the ship and Priya's stomach. She had no idea how fast the ship was sailing, but even in her cell below deck, she thought she could feel the wind blowing through her hair.

The next morning though, the sun did not rise and the sea was once again roiling like a pot of water over a fire. Priya looked out her porthole window and saw that the grey sky was churning, the dark clouds shifting back and forth as though they did not know which way to blow. The waves of the sea grew and lashed against the side of the ship. Priya could hear the sailors above deck as they rushed back and forth, and everyone, not just the captain, was yelling.

The animals below deck shuffled, squawked, and screeched anxiously. They tugged at their chains and shook the bars of their cages. Nabhitha paced in her cage, emitting a low growl. The animals made Priya more nervous than the coming storm itself. Animals had a special sense about this sort of thing, she knew. The fact that the animals were scared told her she needed to be scared as well. She watched out her porthole window as rain suddenly came pouring down and she saw lightning strike the sea.

The ship was tossed about, sending Priya and Nabhitha to the floor of their cells. Water then began pouring down the stairs from the upper deck. The animals shrieked as they too lost their balance or their cages slid across the floor. The ship was knocked hard to one side, and a stack of crates crashed to the ground, smashing open and scattering hundreds of gold coins across the floor. Priya instinctively gathered up the gold coins that rolled into her cage and placed them inside a small bag belted to the inside of her sari. Maybe once they got to Jamaica, she could purchase her own freedom. Maybe she could even buy passage on a ship back to India!

She hardly had time to celebrate her good luck before the ship was shoved the other direction and she was knocked to the floor again, banging her head against the bars of her cage. She wrapped her arms around her head to try and protect herself.

She then heard a loud *snap!* She looked up and saw a crack in the ship's hull, and water was pouring in.

"Help!" she screamed. "Help! We're taking on water!"

Several men rushed down below, including the captain. The men went to work to patch the hull, some holding up planks of wood while others nailed them in place. Still, the water poured in.

"What's going on?" Priya yelled.

"Cyclone!" the captain replied. "Came up suddenly. If we don't get this hull patched—"

The ship was tossed aside again, and Priya felt dizzy and nauseous. It was as though the ship was spinning. All of the men were thrown about and struggled to keep their feet.

The crack in the ship's hull grew larger. The men all ran back toward it, using their hands to hold it together.

"The ship's going to rip apart!" one sailor yelled.

"Keep it together, men!" the captain yelled, but it was too late.

A sound like an explosion ripped through the air. Priya ducked, putting her hands over her head and closing her eyes. There were screams, and then silence, as though everyone, man and beast, was holding their breath, praying they would be spared.

When Priya opened her eyes again, it took her a moment to realize what she was looking at. The mast of the ship seemed to have crashed through the upper deck and was now in the hull. Some men were standing around dumbfounded by what they were seeing. At least one man was dead, impaled by a large wooden shard from the mast. Other men were scattered around on the floor, dazed and disoriented. And there, pinned to the floor of the ship by his leg under the broken mast, was the captain.

"Abandon ship!" she heard someone from up above yell.

That seemed to awaken everyone from their shocked stupor. The men began to move quickly, helping their comrades to their feet and up the stairs out of the hull. No one tried to help the captain.

"What are you doing, you cowards?" the captain yelled. "Help me, you mangy dogs!"

Some of the men paused, but then they ran up the stairs, leaving their captain cursing their names behind them.

"I'll make sure you pay for this!" the captain yelled. "All of you!"

Priya looked up through the hole in the deck and her eyes went wide. The rain poured down and lightning cracked across the sky. The wind howled as the clouds continued to churn. She felt water splash against her legs and looked down. The water was already up to her calves! The ship was sinking! And she was still trapped in her cage.

"Help me!" she screamed as the last of the men who were able climbed up the stairs and out of the hull. A couple of the men looked back at her pitiably, but they knew they couldn't help her if they didn't have the key to her cell.

The key! That was her only way out. She ran over to the captain, who was pinned to the ground close enough that she could reach out and touch his shoulder. His head had lolled to the side and his eyes were closed. The fight he had in him from a moment ago seemed to have gone out of him. She looked at his leg and saw red blood staining the water. He wasn't going to live. He was probably going into shock.

Priya reached through the bars and grabbed the

captain's shoulder, shaking him. "The key!" she yelled. "Give me the key! Help me!"

The captain looked up at her as though in a daze. His eyes were unfocused and he moaned. "What?" he asked.

"The key to my cage!" she said, reaching through and patting his cheek, hoping to wake him up. "Help me! Set me free so I can get out of here!"

The captain took a few deep breaths and then shook his head. "Right," he said. "I'll save you, and then you can help me." He reached into a pocket and produced a keyring, which he handed to her with a shaky hand. Priya did not agree or disagree with his terms as she took the keys from him. He seemed to take it for granted that she would use the precious few moments she had before the ship was completely torn asunder to help him instead of escaping with her life.

She fumbled for a moment as she tried to find the key. She finally found the right key and pulled the door to her cage open. The animals seemed to erupt in cheers as she did so. With no regard for whether the animals might try to scratch or bite her, Priya ran over to the cages and chains and one by one started freeing the animals. None of them tried to hurt her, as if they knew she was their only chance at escape. She had no idea how any of them would survive after the ship sank, but at least they would have a fighting chance.

"What are you doing, you stupid girl?" the captain yelled. "Forget the animals! Save me!"

Priya gave him a hard look. "No," she said. He might not have realized the gravity of the situation, but his leg had been crushed. Without a surgeon to remove the leg and staunch the bleeding immediately he would die. More than that, Priya couldn't even begin to move the mast from off of him. All of the ship's men together could not move a ship's mast. But Priya didn't waste time explaining all this. She knew she couldn't save him, but she wanted him to know that she wouldn't save him even if she could.

She then ran over and unlocked Nabhitha's cage. She pulled the door open and stood behind it, keeping a safe barrier between her and the ferocious tiger. She expected Nabhitha to do like the other animals and quickly escape to the upper deck to try and get off the ship. But she didn't.

Nabhitha stalked over toward the captain, deftly climbing over the mast toward her prey. She growled as she bared her fangs at him.

Priya turned away and started to run up the stairs. She had done the right thing in freeing the tiger, but she couldn't free the captain. It was no concern of hers what the tiger chose to do with her chance to escape. In fact, killing the captain might be a mercy. Otherwise he was only going to drown when the ship sank anyway.

But as she started to climb the stairs, something tugged at her. She remembered the horror of seeing the man who tried to rape her ripped apart by Nabhitha's claws and teeth. She knew that no matter how evil the captain was, no one deserved to die in such a manner. She turned back as Nabhitha's growled in the captain's face.

"No!" he cried, nearly weeping.

"Nabhitha!" Priya yelled. "Stop! Let's go!" She had no reason to think the tiger would listen to her. It was a tiger! Nabhitha would do as she pleased. But to her surprise, Nabhitha stopped, turned around, and then fled up the stairs to the upper deck.

Priya felt her chest flutter with fear for a moment as Nabhitha charged past her. Even though Nabhitha had started to act friendly toward her when they were in their cages, she knew better than to ever underestimate Nabhitha's ferocity again. She breathed a sigh of relief as Nabhitha passed her by, nearly flying up the stairs. But she almost laughed to herself when she heard several screams from up above as the sailors saw the tiger emerge.

"You'll never make it," the captain said, his voice despondent. "The ship, the storm, the sea itself. You'll be ripped apart and never make it to shore. You're as dead as me, girl."

"If I live longer than you," Priya said, "I'll have lived long enough." She then turned and climbed up the stairs, out of the ship's hull.

CHAPTER ELEVEN

*T*he deck was in chaos. The wind and rain whipped around Priya and she struggled to see or even stand upright. A man ran by, knocking her to the deck, but he didn't seem to even take notice of her. On her hands and knees, she crawled over to the ship's railing and hung on for dear life.

All around her, the wind roared. She had been through some powerful storms in her life, but nothing like this. And she had always been in the safety of her home, in the warmth of her mother's arms when a storm passed by. The salty sea air caused her feet and her grip to slip and she feared that at any moment she would be tossed into the unforgiving ocean below. She had never been so frightened.

Even though the salt water stung, she opened her eyes to see what was happening around her. She watched as some of the animals and men jumped over the side of the ship. She had no idea why. Wasn't it safer here, out of the water? She saw some of the birds open their wings and try to fly away, but they were quickly lost from her sight in the wind and clouds. Other animals and men were like Priya, hunkering down and trying to hold on and ride out the storm. But as she felt her feet slip behind her, she could feel that the ship was still sinking. Even if the storm miraculously stopped, they would soon all be lost, alone on the water.

She didn't see Nabhitha anywhere.

She felt the ship tip further and her feet continued to slip out from under her. She needed to move. Find something more secure to hold onto. She grabbed onto whatever she could to help her move toward the middle of the ship where several men were huddled together.

"Help me!" she yelled, but to her own ears, in the howl of the storm, it sounded like little more than a whisper. But some of the men did hear her and looked at her in surprise. One of the men stretched his hand toward her. She reached for it, straining against the wind and rain to reach him.

She heard what sounded like the crack of a whip. She looked up and saw several ropes that had snapped waving in through the air.

"Look out!" a voice rang out, but it was too late. The pylon the ropes had been holding in place was falling toward her, swinging at a great speed as one lone rope still held it fast.

She put her arms in front of her to brace for the blow and held her breath. The force from the impact was like being hit with a cannonball. It knocked the breath from her lungs and she felt herself flying backward. She expected to hit the railing, but she didn't. She just kept falling, and falling, and falling.

She felt as though she had fallen into a bucket of needles as she slammed into the ocean that had once been below her. The pain and the cold rushed through her skin and into her very bones. It hurt so much, she couldn't move, she could only feel herself sinking, the world turning dark and silent. But then, she started to float upward, and slowly she felt feeling return to her limbs. She kicked her legs and waved her arms, pushing herself back toward the surface.

As she emerged from the water, she took a deep breath. Then another, and another. She coughed and sputtered, but she was alive. Somehow, she was still alive.

She looked around, trying to figure out what to do now. If she should go back to the ship or try to find some sort of raft. She looked at the ship and saw that it was sitting at an impossible angle, with the bow of the ship slowly rising into the air.

She then heard a great moaning sound. A groaning. Like the cry of despair from a hundred elephants. She then heard the same cracking sound she had heard before the ship began taking on water and she realized the ship was snapping in two. She looked up and saw the last of the men who had been on the deck jumping into the water and doing their best to swim away. She tried to follow suit, but she was not a strong swimmer, and as the boat sank under the water, she could feel herself being sucked under as well.

She screamed even though it would do her no good. She took a deep breath and was dragged under.

She flailed about, trying helplessly to get back to the surface or grab onto something that would help her float. But she could feel nothing. Nothing except the current that was still tugging at her, pulling her deeper and deeper. She could feel herself growing weak with exhaustion. The pressure on her skull was painful. And her lungs burned, begging for air. She knew she was going to die.

She prayed to the gods one last time. But not to be spared. She knew her life was lost. She prayed for her parents. That the customs official would tell them he had seen her alive, on a ship bound for the Americas. She prayed they would take comfort in knowing that their daughter survived and was living a new life far away. Even if they would never see her again, they could take comfort in believing that she was alive and safe, maybe even living a good life, somehow. Somewhere.

She felt something brush by her fingers. With the last of her strength, she closed her hands around it tightly. She brought her other hand over and gripped the mysterious object with that hand as well. She then felt the thing move and take her with it. Slowly, slowly, bit by bit, she could feel the object taking her through the water and up toward the surface.

When she broke through the water and took a breath, she realized that she was clutching Nabhitha's fur! At first, she started, releasing her grip. But Nabhitha seemed to send her a look of warning, telling her to hold on. In her daze after nearly drowning, Priya did not try to make sense of what was happening. She draped her arms over Nabhitha's back and held on tightly.

Nabhitha then swam away from the ship quickly. She was a powerful swimmer and in only a moment, she was well away from the sinking ship. After a few more breaths, Priya looked up and saw that Nabhitha was heading toward a longboat. Some of the men must have managed to release them before the ship went down.

"He...help me," Priya muttered weakly as they neared the boat. Two men looked out of the boat down at her, but they quickly backed up when they saw Nabhitha.

Nabhitha growled at them and grabbed onto the side of the boat with her paws, her claws extended. Her weight tipped the boat sideways and the men screamed. One of them grabbed an oar and tried to hit Nabhitha over the head with it, but that just made Nabhitha angrier. She growled and put all her weight on the side of the boat, tipping it further and enabling her to slide half of herself up into it. The men screamed and jumped into the water.

Priya grabbed the side of the vessel and pulled herself off of Nabhitha's back and into the boat. Nabhitha then pulled the rest of her body into the boat. Priya collapsed to the floor as Nabhitha crouched down at the other end. Priya looked up at the sky as the rain fell on her face. The clouds were no longer churning and she could no longer hear thunder. The worst of the storm had passed.

And she was alive.

The ship had sunk, but she was safe in a boat with only a gentle rain falling on her. She felt tears flow out of her eyes. Tears of gratitude for whatever goddess had seen her worthy to be spared this day.

She felt exhaustion settle over her body and she gave herself over to it. She let herself fall asleep with no thought to the fact that there were no longer iron bars between her and the ferocious Nabhitha.

CHAPTER TWELVE

*P*riya woke to the warmth of the sun baking her brown skin. She opened her eyes and was nearly blinded by the bright sunlight. Was it the same day? Or the next one? Or the one after that? She had no idea if she had slept for a few minutes or several days. It took her a moment to remember everything that had happened. The terrible storm. The ship splintering. The captain trapped under the broken mast. Almost drowning. Nabhitha rescuing her.

Nabhitha!

Priya sat up quickly. At the other end of the small boat, Nabhitha sat licking the salt water off her paws, emitting a low rumbling sound. Priya felt a small sense of panic rising up in her stomach. Wait. Was that panic? She felt sick. She put her head over the side of the boat and retched up salt water into the sea. Then she retched again. Again and again until there was only bile left and the taste of seawater on her tongue. She must have swallowed quite a bit after she fell off the ship. She felt a little dizzy, so she sat down in the boat, laying her head back and looking at Nabhitha, who seemed to pay her no mind.

She should be dreaming. She was on a boat with a tiger. Her mother would never believe such a thing. It was like a story from the *Mahbharata*, the great Indian epic. She then remembered how she had prayed for salvation, for a way home. Could the gods have sent the storm? And guided Nabhitha to save her? Ugh! No! That was even more ludicrous. Why would the gods take note of her? Just a stupid girl who got herself into this mess. It was all just...just a series of terrible events.

Nabhitha stood, stretched, and then sat in a new position where she could clean the saltwater off a different part of her body.

Priya started to relax. Nabhitha was obviously unconcerned about Priya's presence. Priya knew better than to turn her back on Nabhitha, but she thought that if Nabhitha was going to eat her, she'd have done it by now.

Or she might eat her later if she got hungry enough.

Priya moved from the bottom of the boat to one of the planks that served as seating. She looked all around them and saw nothing but ocean in every direction. There were no ships or any hint of land anywhere. Well, she did see several crates and a few shards of wood floating about. The only remnants of the once great ship that had threatened to carry her away. The ship—and all the men and animals and goods that had once been on it—were gone. Only Priya and Nabhitha remained. Well, she supposed it was possible that other longboats of sailors might have escaped as well, but they were nowhere in sight.

She looked in the bottom of the boat to see if there were any supplies. She found four oars and some fishing supplies, including a net, a spear, and some fishing poles. She picked up one of the oars first and stuck it in the water. She made a paddling motion, but it took far more effort than she ever imagined and they barely moved. Nabhitha made a chuffing sound and cocked her head.

"You could help me, you know," Priya told her. "You probably weigh ten times more than I do!"

Nabhitha snuffled at the insult, but made no move to help. She might have been a powerful swimmer, but she was useless at paddling a boat.

Priya tried paddling again a few more times, but she was using far too much energy and making no progress. She had no food and no water. She needed to conserve her strength. But how were they going to make it back to land? As she looked around, she realized paddling might not get them any closer to land anyway. She didn't know which direction to go. She might just make things worse by paddling the wrong way. She supposed the best thing to do for now was to just sit and wait. Eventually, they would drift closer to land, or she would see birds, who would never fly far from a tree to land on, or a ship would pass by. At some point, she would see something that would indicate the right way to go.

Or they would sit in the boat until they died.

If they didn't find water, death would come rather quickly. In only a couple of days, Priya thought. She wondered if there was a way to strain the salt out of the salt-water that surrounded them. Of course, if there was a way to do that, she was sure she would have heard of it. There would never be a drought again if people were able to make drinking water out of salt water.

Maybe she could work on finding food. She couldn't

remember when she last ate, and she had thrown up so much, she was rather hungry. Maybe the moisture inside some fish they could catch and eat would help sustain them. She looked at Nabhitha out of the corner of her eye. Nabhitha might be calm now, but who knew what she might do if she got hungry.

Priya was not a very experienced fisher; she didn't need to fish to survive back in Bombay. If the Parker family, or even her own family, wanted fish, they just bought them in the market. She had been fishing with her cousins in the river a few times when she had gone to visit them, but it had only been for fun. She knew the basic premise, how to bait a hook and drop it in the water. But she didn't have anything she could use for bait. There were also a spear and net in the boat. She wondered if those might be more useful.

She picked up the spear to examine it, trying to figure out if there was a trick to using it. The spear was multi-pronged and looked rather nasty, as though it was designed to both stab the fish and grip hold of it. She imagined it must be rather painful to be caught by one.

As she was looking at it, she heard Nabhitha growl behind her, and her heart froze. She slowly turned and saw that Nabhitha was in a crouch, her fangs bared.

"Nabhitha," she whispered, her voice quavering. "What...what is it?"

Nabhitha continued to growl and crouched lower. Priya tried to figure out what had Nabhitha so upset when she realized that Nabhitha wasn't looking at her, but at the spear. She remembered how the captain had stabbed Nabhitha with the sharpened stick to stop her from eating the man who had attacked her. Now that Nabhitha saw

Priya holding the spear, she must have thought Priya might use it on her as well.

"It's okay," Priya whispered. "I'm...just...gonna..." She slowly moved her arm out over the water. Nabhitha did not take her eyes off the spear. Priya then opened her hand and let the spear fall into the water. "See. It's gone. I'm not going to hurt you, okay?"

Nabhitha seemed dubious, but she stopped growling and sat up from her crouch. But she didn't go back to cleaning herself. Instead, she sat and watched Priya with renewed interest.

Priya exhaled, glad to still be alive. She needed to be more careful, more conscious of Nabhitha's feelings if she wanted to have any hope of surviving in this boat with her.

And she still needed to figure out how to feed them.

She still had a net and a fishing pole. She decided to see if any of their dumb luck held out and tossed the netting out into the sea. She watched it sink, then she dragged it back to the boat.

To her surprise, she did manage to snag a couple of tiny fish, about the side of her finger.

"What do you think?" Priya asked Nabhitha as she held up the fish. "Are we going to eat like kings tonight?"

Nabhitha snuffled her disappointment. Priya tossed the net out again and pulled it back. Again, she caught only a couple of tiny fish.

"I think the bigger fish must hang about in deeper water," Priya said as she leaned over the side and looked down. "If only we had some bait, we could—" She paused, then she laughed at herself. "But now we do have bait!" She picked up one of the little fish. "Forgive me," she said to the little fish as she quickly stabbed a hook through its side.

Then she dropped the line into the water and let it out. She then held her breath as they waited.

When she felt a little tug on the line, she was so excited she nearly squealed. Then she remembered that she needed to be calm in case Nabhitha was still on edge. She reeled the line back in at a steady pace even though her fingers were shaking with anticipation. She watched the water as she pulled the line up. She couldn't stop smiling as she saw the shimmering glint of scales coming toward her.

"I did it!" she exclaimed when she pulled the fish, as long as her arm and very fat, into the boat. She held the fish up proudly for Nabhitha to see. Nabhitha sat up with interest, nearly licking her lips at the sight. "Oh, of course." Priya was more than willing to give the first catch of the day to the hungry tiger she shared her boat with. She worked the hook out of the fish's mouth and then tossed the fish to Nabhitha.

Nabhitha grabbed at the fish with her paw and ate it in two bites. She then sat back and cocked her head at Priya, as though asking for more.

Priya smiled and baited the hook with another one of the tiny fish. She pulled up four more fat fish and gave three of them to Nabhitha. She had been so excited over the prospect of catching fish, she hadn't thought ahead enough to how she would have to kill and eat the fish herself. And she would have to eat it raw.

Priya had never killed an animal before. Indians rarely ate meat, but when they did, slaughtering was usually considered men's work. Her father would kill a fish, for example, quickly and humanely, and she and her mother would prepare and cook it. But here on the boat, she didn't have a knife or hatchet to dispatch of the head, and of course she had no way to clean the fish or cook it.

She quickly lost her appetite. She was about to toss her

fish to Nabhitha when she realized that she *needed* to eat the fish. She needed the sustenance and the moisture. If she didn't eat the fish, she would die. Then Nabhitha would eat her. And then Nabhitha would die without someone to fish for her.

Priya sighed and lamented how cruel and unfair the world was, then she did what had to be done.

CHAPTER THIRTEEN

*E*very inch of Priya's skin hurt. Her once brown skin was now a deep red. She felt as though she was roasting. There was no shade in the boat to protect her from the sun. She had lost her sari wrap in the ocean and, of course, hadn't grabbed any of the supplies from her room. She had little more than a choli around her breasts and dhoti wrapped around her waist and legs. She unwrapped her dhoti and covered different areas of her body when she could, but something was always exposed. She tried pouring water over herself, and even jumping into the ocean a few times—always while keeping a careful hold on the boat—to try and cool off and give her skin some relief, but the salt in the water was drying her skin out, causing the burned skin to crack and bleed, which made the salt-water even more painful to touch.

Nabhitha was in a similar pathetic state. Priya didn't know if tigers could get a sunburn, but the sunlight and heat were definitely upsetting the tiger. All day, Nabhitha sat with her head on her paws, panting and looking long-ingly out over the water, as though she could will land to appear. She barely moved during the heat of the day, but she ate eagerly in the evenings when Priya forced herself to fish.

They were both exhausted and losing hope.

"I'm sorry, Nabhitha," Priya said. She wasn't sure why she was apologizing. She might have gotten herself into this mess when she went to Lord Fullerton's house, but she had nothing to do with Nabhitha getting captured. She also didn't have anything to do with the storm or getting them stranded on this little boat. Without Priya, Nabhitha would have gone down with the ship. Still, apologizing seemed to be the only thing she could think to say. Nabhitha looked at Priya out of the corner of her eye without moving her head and made a little grunt, but otherwise did not acknowledge her.

Perhaps Priya was hoping her apology reached the people who needed it the most—her parents. Whether she lived one more day or a hundred years, she would never forgive herself for the pain she caused them. She was glad they would not know she had died like this, but even if they thought she was alive, she was still lost to them forever, and they would always ache from that loss.

She thought about how her mother taught her to pray, to kneel before the family altar and burn incense and recite the mantras. Then she would sit on her mother's lap and listen to the stories about warrior goddesses and hero kings. Her father wasn't around much, but she knew he loved her. Many times, late at night, long after she had fallen asleep, she would awake with his hand petting her hair and his voice saying how proud of her he was. Even though she didn't see him often, she always felt he was there in spirit, guiding and protecting her.

She had always dreamed of one day making enough

money that they wouldn't have to slave away for the Parker family anymore. She had hoped to care for them in their old age. They didn't have any other children. Who would now care for them when they were too old to work? Priya's body was too dry to shed any more tears, but if she could cry for anything, it would be for failing in her filial duty to care for her parents one day.

Priya had pulled her dhoti over her face and hunkered down into the boat to try and sleep through the day when she heard Nabhitha chuffing. Priya looked up and saw that Nabhitha had raised her head and was panting hard, as though she was looking at something. Then, Priya heard it.

Overhead, a seagull flew by, cawing all the way. Priya shot up and looked at the water. Floating nearby was a seagull, happily taking a bath. Nabhitha squirmed, obviously hungry for something other than fish. Priya wondered if she could use the net to catch the seagull and feed it to Nabhitha. But then she realized that if there were seagulls about, then there had to be...

Land!

Priya nearly screamed in her excitement when she saw a brown haze in the distance.

"Nabhitha!" Priya said, pointing. "Look! A beach! We are saved." Priya shook her head, surprised that land was not the first thing she thought of when she saw the birds, but she thought that the sun must have fried her brain as well as her skin.

Nabhitha sat up and looked anxiously at the shore. She looked at Priya and whined, as though begging for her to somehow get them to that land as quickly as possible.

Priya thought about what to do. The land was still quite far away, probably farther away than she realized. She didn't think even Nabhitha could swim that far without passing out from exhaustion. She still had the paddles, but she knew from experience that she wouldn't be able to get them much closer under her own pitiful strength.

"It's okay, Nabhitha," Priya said. "The ocean has brought us this far. We just need to be patient and hope that the current will continue to move us toward the shore."

Nabhitha sat back down but continued to whine. She then seemed to remember the nearby bird. She looked at it and licked her lips, anxiously shifting from one foot to the other.

Priya thought that if she wanted to keep Nabhitha from leaping out of the boat, she needed to give her something to tide her over. She picked up the net and waited until the bird wasn't looking before tossing it out.

"I'm sorry, friend," Priya said as she untangled the bird from the net. "Your sacrifice is greatly appreciated." Then she tossed the bird to Nabhitha and turned her head away as Nabhitha eagerly ate.

*P*riya and Nabhitha watched for hours as the shoreline slowly crept closer. They didn't see anything that looked like a city, and Priya wondered if they were drifting around a remote island. They could be anywhere within a few days of sailing from Goa. The ship had only sailed for a day and a night, but they had been drifting for several more. She didn't think it was possible that they could have drifted as far away as Africa or Indonesia, but there were countless islands in the ocean. They could be anywhere. When day turned into night, they were still much too far from the shore to try and reach it, and they couldn't see anything at night, so all they could do was wait for the next day. Priya prayed that they did not drift away from the land in the night and end up in the empty sea again. She didn't think that they would live much longer if that happened.

Neither of them slept very well that night. They both looked out of the boat in the direction they had last seen the shore and waited anxiously for the sun to rise.

They were not disappointed.

"There it is!" Priya said, jumping up as soon as there was enough light to see. The shore was much closer now. It was still too far away to swim, but they were certainly closer.

Nabhitha stood with her paws on the edge of the boat and leaned as far forward as she could.

"It won't be long now," Priya said. "By the end of the day, we will—" She screamed as a wave rolled up under them, knocking them both off balance and back into the boat. She sat back up and held on tightly as the boat rocked from side to side and then settled.

"What happened?" she asked, even though she knew that Nabhitha couldn't answer. She looked at the shore and thought it was a little farther away now, but she didn't know why or how.

They sat in the boat and waited as they started to drift closer to the land. But then it happened again! A wave rolled up and pushed them back out to sea.

Priya grunted in frustration. She remembered when she was on the ship, how it rocked violently as they pulled away from the port. Once they were out at sea, the ocean, and the ship, calmed. In the distance, she watched as waves broke upon the shore. She tried to recall ever learning anything about the ocean from her classes or her parents, but her mind was blank. She could only assume that the ocean had brought them as close to shore as possible. As the gentle sea turned into crashing waves, the boat was pushed away from the land instead of closer to it.

"Don't worry, Nabhitha," Priya said as she pulled out her paddle. "We haven't come this far just to sit here and do nothing."

The next time a wave rolled up under them, Priya used her paddle to try and cut through the water, like making a path to the shore. To her surprise, it worked! They weren't any closer to the shore, but they weren't any farther away from it either.

"Is that progress?" Priya asked the tiger. "I think that was progress."

Priya used her paddle with the next wave, but it took considerably more effort to hold the paddle straight. But it did work, and now they were slightly closer to the shore.

"Just...just wait," Priya panted. "We...we will get there."

With the next wave, Priya held her paddle with all her strength, her feet hooked under the paneled seats to keep from falling over. She grunted with the exertion the task required, but then she gasped and fell forward, nearly tipping out of the boat as the current sucked the paddle from her hands, under the boat. Priya fell back as the wave then knocked them back where they were before.

"By the gods!" Priya cursed, screaming at the ocean as she went to the other side of the boat and watched her paddle drift away. Priya looked back at the shore, a lump forming in her chest at the thought that it was so close, and yet so far.

Nabhitha had finally had enough. She leaped into the water and swam for shore so quickly and easily, she moved like a shark with only her head peeking above the water. In moments, she was halfway to the shore.

Priya knew she had no choice but to follow. She knew

she probably wouldn't make it, but there was no other option. If she stayed in the boat and ended up stranded at sea, she would die. Her only chance at survival was getting to the land.

She tied her dhoti tightly and then jumped into the sea. She kicked her legs and thrashed her arms to stay above water, which was not easy as the water rolled around her. She then aimed for the shore and kicked and kicked. After several minutes, she knew she wasn't making any progress. The shore still looked the same. She looked back and saw that the boat had been pushed back out to calmer sea waters. There was no way she could reach it either at this point.

Priya moaned as she rolled onto her back and just did her best to keep her head above water. She whimpered as water got into her eyes and mouth and open wounds. She wondered if this was at least better than dying on a slave ship or in bondage in a foreign land and decided that it was. Of course, given the choice, she'd rather not die at all. But in this moment, as she felt her strength go out of her and she floated listlessly, she supposed there were worse ways to go.

She felt something touch her leg and she gasped. *Shark!* she thought. She pulled her legs up, but then she felt the creature swim up under her and lift her higher in the water. She lowered her hands and placed them on the creature's back. She knew what it was.

"Nabhitha!" she cried as the tiger's head popped out of the water. Nabhitha pulled Priya along on her back toward the shore. Priya kissed the top of Nabhitha's head. "My dearest friend! Thank you! For this life and hundred after it, thank you!"

Nabhitha did not swim as elegantly as before. In fact, she seemed to struggle a bit, panting and slowing before pushing herself harder. But quickly, the land grew closer. If Priya could have cried tears of happiness, she would have.

Finally, Nabhitha's feet touched the sand under the water and she was able to climb out of the ocean with Priya on her back. Once the water was shallow enough, Priya rolled off of Nabhitha and kissed the ground. She then thanked the gods for her salvation, and she blessed Nabhitha.

Priya crawled across the hot sand to the tree line and to the much-needed shade. She looked around and saw Nabhitha, panting as she stared out at the sea. Priya wondered what the tiger was thinking. Was she as grateful as Priya that they had somehow managed to survive?

Nabhitha then looked at Priya, and Priya knew it was for the last time. Together, they had survived, but now, Nabhitha was free. She was a tiger, and she needed to go her own way.

"Thank you," Priya said one more time. Nabhitha chuffed, then she turned and ran into the jungle.

Priya laid down and fell asleep, thankful for her hero tiger.

CHAPTER FOURTEEN

*P*riya awoke and wiped the sand from her face. She had no idea how long she had slept, but she felt rested. It had been horribly uncomfortable sleeping on the little boat. It was hard to sleep at all, but when she did she woke up in every sort of pain. Here on the shore, she had been able to stretch out and not worry about the sun beating down on her.

She sat up and looked out at the sea, the gentle waves rolling up the shore. The air smelled fresh and clean and she dug her toes into the warm sand. It was so peaceful here, not another human in sight. Only the sounds of the crashing waves and cawing birds could be heard. For the first time in longer than she could remember, she was at peace. She raised her face to the sky and thanked the gods once again for saving her. She was alive. She was free. She didn't know where she was, but at least she was not in America or England. Wherever she was, she was not far from home. Of that she was certain.

She had hope.

Once she found people, she could find out where she

was and then find her way home. She knew there would still be difficulties ahead. She had no money, no food, no clothes. She was lost and alone. But sitting here wouldn't improve her situation. She needed to get moving and figure out a plan.

She stood up and stretched. She was hungry and thirsty. She started to wander into the woods, but she winced when she stepped on a burr. She knew she had been wearing shoes on the ship, but they were long gone now. She needed to find some sort of footwear. A new sari wouldn't go amiss either, and she couldn't even imagine how abhorrent her hair must have looked. Her hair was normally long and thick. Her mother would help her brush her hair out every night before bed, and at least once a week she would have to wash it and oil it to keep it strong and healthy. She couldn't see her hair, but she knew it was terribly matted and caked with salt and sand.

She looked toward the water and saw there was a lot of rubbish along the shore. Mainly splinters of planks, but she could see there were some crates and barrels. She wondered if they were remains from the shipwreck. If so, she knew the ship had lots of quality merchandise on board. She might be able to find some things that would be of use to her. She stepped out of the shade and onto the sand, and she immediately ran back into the shade. The sand was like walking on hot coals!

She looked around and debated what to do. She supposed she could wait until the sun set. But as she looked up at the sun, high in the sky, she knew it would be a long time before that happened, and she would rather not wait. She looked back to the woods and saw several large palm fronds on the ground. She wrapped them around her feet and used some long thick pieces of grass to secure them.

She almost laughed at how ridiculous she surely looked. But as she stepped out onto the sun and discovered that her makeshift "shoes" worked, she felt more than a little proud.

As she walked along the shore, she was surprised at the amount of debris, but most of it was useless. Broken planks and worn ropes littered the beach. She found an empty barrel and wondered if it had been used to hold rainwater at some point. She came across a crate that was cracked open, and as she moved it, hundreds of sticks of cinnamon poured out. They smelled fantastic, which made her stomach rumble, but there was little they could do to ease her hunger or thirst.

Even though her leaf shoes, her feet were getting hot on the sand, so she wandered down to the water to cool them off. As she walked along the water's edge, she came across several small items that had become tangled in a net— including a canteen.

She opened it and to her surprise it was full of water. She fell to her knees as she drank the water, putting her lips around the opening so as not to lose a single drop. She relished the taste of the first fresh water she had drunk in days. She knew she should probably ration it, but her body wouldn't let her. She drank every drop, and still her body begged for more. She panted, catching her breath after not even stopping to breathe as she drank. She was once again out of water. But that was okay. Once she finished scavenging the beach she could head into the woods and find a freshwater source. And now that she had her canteen, she wouldn't need to worry about finding water again.

As she continued walking, she saw a heap of...something further down the beach. She couldn't quite make out what it was until she got closer. She finally realized that it was a body.

Her first instinct was to run away and hide. She had been attacked by too many men lately to take any chances with her safety now that Nabhitha was gone. She ducked behind an empty, smashed crate and watched for a moment. The body only moved when the waves washed over him, and he was laying at an unnatural angle. Surely, he was dead. Still, she grabbed a broken stick and held it in front of her as she approached. She poked him with her stick, but he did not move or utter a sound.

"Hey!" she yelled, and then waited. "Hey, you!" she said again, poking him harder with her stick. She then moved around the other side to try and get a look at his face. But when she saw it, she almost wished she hadn't.

It was the man who had been tasked with watching her after Nabhitha killed the man who attacked her. The one who had said he was friends with her would-be rapist. She knew it was wrong, but she was glad he was dead. But his eyes were open and his mouth was agape in a never-ending yet silent scream. His face was as pale as a ghost. It was a gruesome sight, so she turned away, walking back around him so she didn't have to see that twisted contortion of a face. She nearly walked away when she realized he was still wearing his boots.

It was morbid, she knew, and possibly sacrilegious, but she was in desperate need of shoes. Once she started traveling, who knew what she might come across. If she needed to run from bad people or dangerous animals, she would need sturdy shoes. This man was already dead, but her life could depend on taking the boots. She took a deep breath and removed the man's boots. She then sat down and put them on her own feet. They were a little big for her, but she pulled the laces tight. As she got up to leave, she noticed that the man also had a large knife tucked into a sheath and belted around his waist. She gritted her teeth, unlatched the belt, and pulled the knife and sheath from his body, then belted it around her own waist. She then gave the man a small nod and continued her walk down the beach.

She rifled through some more debris as she walked, but she didn't find anything else of use until she came to a large crate that was nearly intact. She used her knife to pry some of the boards loose and thanked the gods when she found dozens of bolts of silk.

The silks were incredibly soft and in some of the most vibrant colors she'd ever seen. She pulled out one of a mottled green color—she didn't want to stand out too much while she was traveling—and cut a piece a few meters long, long enough to wrap around her properly. She also cut a long thin piece and used it to wrap her hair. She then cut a few extra pieces for good measure. You never knew when a length of cloth might come in handy. She tied one piece into a bag and put the other pieces and the canteen inside it.

She was still a long way from having her needs met, but she had shoes, clothes, a way to carry water, and a weapon, which was more than she had when she washed up on the shore. She felt she had earned a break, so she went back to the tree line and walked to where she had slept overnight. The spot didn't really offer any more comfort or protection than any other place she could have chosen along the edge of the jungle, but it was familiar and gave her a sense of balance as she tried to orient herself.

As she approached her spot, she saw something that had not been there before. A dead rabbit. At first, she was alarmed. Who could have left it? Were there other people around? Was it a warning? Then she heard a low growling sound emitting from the jungle.

Nabhitha was still watching her.

So, the tiger had not abandoned her after all. She was still there, protecting her, and now providing for her as well.

She nearly laughed. Apparently, this amma tiger had taken Priya under her paw. Priya had fed Nabhitha in the boat. Maybe Nabhitha was returning the favor. She was almost sad she couldn't eat the rabbit. She had no fire to cook it over. Still, she was grateful. She used her knife to skin and gut the rabbit and she rinsed it off in the seawater. She then tied the carcass to her belt. She decided that there was still plenty of daylight left and she didn't want to waste it. She needed to find people. A village. Anything. If she could find people, maybe she could offer to share her rabbit with them if they shared their fire with her. Then she could learn where she was and come up with a plan for getting home.

"Thank you, Nabhitha," she said as she walked, and this time, she knew the tiger was not far behind.

CHAPTER FIFTEEN

*P*riya remembered that she needed to find water before she trekked too far, and she wouldn't find any here on the beach. So she went into the jungle. Even though it had been bright and sunny on the beach, after only a few steps into the jungle it was dark and cool. The trees were thick and luscious, blocking out most of the sun. The air here was fresh and clean, but in a different way from the clean beach air. The trees seemed to filter out most of the salt, so the air was crisp and refreshing. If she didn't find a village tonight, she would have to find somewhere in the jungle to sleep.

As she walked, she felt as though she was being watched, and she glanced over her shoulder repeatedly. She hoped it was Nabhitha. She couldn't see or hear her, but she didn't feel as though she was in any danger from whoever might be there.

She hadn't walked far when she heard a trickling sound. She followed it and found a small creek that fed into a pool. She dropped her bag and fell to her knees as she dipped her hands into the water. The water was cool and sweet as she brought it to her mouth. She drank and drank and felt as though she could never drink enough. When her stomach was finally full, she took off her clothes and climbed into the pool. She sank under the water, allowing her body to absorb the water through her skin. Her burned skin and parched lips thanked her as they stopped aching for the first time in days. She hadn't realized how much constant pain her body had been in until she stopped hurting. She dreaded getting out of the water, but she was in no rush, so she soaked in the water until she started to grow cold.

She washed her hair as thoroughly as she could without soap and rinsed the salt and sand out of every nook and crevice before climbing back out. She tossed away her old dhoti and used a new strip of silk instead. But as the old dhoti hit the ground, she heard it clink and she remembered that she had put some gold coins in the pocket. She pulled out the coins and held them in her hand for a moment, watching them gleam as they burned hotly in her hand. There had been crates of gold on that ship. Gold stolen from the Indian people, though the British called them "taxes." But the money wasn't used to improve the lives of Indian people, it was shipped back to England to improve lives there. But in the end, all that gold, all that opium, the spices, the silk, the smuggled animals and slaves couldn't save the dozens of men who had been on that ship. They all died—and only Priya remained.

She smirked at that as she put the gold into her bag.

She kept her old choti, since she didn't have a replacement for that, but she washed it out as best she could before putting it back on. She wrapped the green silk around her shoulders, put on her boots, wrapped her hair, picked up her skinned rabbit, and then resumed walking, feeling fresh and clean for the first time in days.

*I*t was nearly dark by the time she saw signs of a village. She saw a boy tending to his goats. She could smell the smoke from fires. And she could hear voices and laughter from somewhere nearby. She asked the boy the way to the village and he pointed to a trail that led through the jungle. She thanked him and followed it. But she had not gotten far when she heard a rustling sound in the underbrush and muffled voices. Voices that sounded angry.

As she got closer, she heard stifled crying and more angry words. They were the sounds of a man and woman, and Priya's heart grew hot. When she finally found them, she was not surprised by what she saw.

A white man in a British uniform had pinned an Indian girl to a tree. His hand was over her mouth, but tears were streaming down her face. With his other hand, he had the girl's sari hitched up nearly to her waist and he was pounding her with his hips.

Priya was blinded by her rage. Without thinking she ran forward, using the whole weight of her body to push the man away. In his shock, the man was knocked to the ground.

"You monster!" Priya screamed at him.

The man shook his head and looked up, his eyes wide in shock at the sight of her. Then his mouth twisted into a snarl. "You'll pay for that, darkie!"

Priya pulled out her knife and held it in front of her. "You're the one who will pay!" she screamed.

The man jumped up and lunged at her. Priya brought her knife down, but he blocked it easily, knocking the knife from her hand. Then he slapped her so hard across the face, her neck popped. He pushed her to the ground, and the back of her head hit the dirt hard, causing her vision to spin. He tried to pin her arms down, but her hands—dry from the saltwater—easily slipped from his grasp and she slapped and clawed at his face.

"I'm going to kill you!" the man yelled as he grabbed both of her small wrists in one of his large hands and finally pinned her to the ground. He then started to fumble with her sari.

"No!" Priya screamed. "No!"

Priya wasn't sure which came first—the scream from the man or the roar from the tiger. Nabhitha seemed to come out of nowhere as she leaped over Priya, knocking the man to the ground and then dragging him deep into the woods. Priya sat up, panting, her eyes wide. She hadn't even considered that Nabhitha would save her, even though she had done it before. She had stupidly thought she could fight the man on her own.

The other girl's screaming broke Priya out of her thoughts. Priya jumped up and took the girl in her arms. She grabbed her knife from where it had fallen to the ground and then ushered the girl along the trail and into the village.

The screaming and blubbering from the girl brought many people toward them as they walked into the village, both Indians and British soldiers. It seemed to Priya that there were far more British soldiers here than was normal.

"What happened?" someone asked.

"A soldier was raping her," Priya said. "I knocked him away. Tried to fight him."

"Who was it?" one of the soldiers asked.

"I...I don't know," Priya said.

"Well, what did he look like?" the soldier pressed.

"I...umm...light hair, light skin," she said. "It doesn't matter. He's dead. A tiger killed him."

The people let out a collective gasp.

"You," the soldier, who Priya realized was the commanding officer, said, pointing to another soldier. "Gather the men. We have a dangerous tiger to find."

"What?" Priya asked, still holding tightly to the girl. "That tiger saved our lives. He would have killed us both."

"Hmm, says you," the commander said with an air of disdain. "How do I know you didn't try to lure him into the woods with promises of sex just to kill and rob him?"

"What?" Priya nearly screamed. "Are you out of your mind? He was raping this girl!"

"I'll be the judge of that," the man said. "Just as soon as we find the remains of our comrade and dispatch the tiger."

"This is ridiculous—" Priya said.

"My daughter!" a woman cried, cutting Priya off as she made her way through the crowd. "My precious baby."

The woman's words made Priya's heart ache for her own mother. She let the girl go, only to watch her collapse into the arms of her mother.

"My darling," the mother cried. "What happened? Are you all right?"

The girl could not speak, but she shook her head as she cried.

"She is alive," Priya said. "It could have been much worse."

A man came up beside Priya and took her hands, squeezing them tightly. "You have brought out daughter home to us. Please, come to our house." Then he leaned in and whispered in her ear so the soldier couldn't hear him, "We can speak more freely there."

Priya nodded and followed the family to a small hut.

They all went inside where a fire was burning and the woman seemed to have been in the middle of boiling rice for dinner which was now burning, filling the hut with smoke. Priya ran over and removed the pot. She could tell that the mother did not want to let her daughter out of her arms for even a moment.

"Thank you!" the mother said to Priya as she sat next to her daughter on a crude wooden couch. "You are such a capable girl! Your own mother must be very proud of you."

"I...I am a long way from home," Priya said honestly.

"Please, give me a few minutes, then I will find something for you to eat as thanks," the mother said.

Priya then remembered her rabbit. She unhooked it from her belt and held it up to the father. "I'm sorry. I was looking for someone to share this rabbit with. It's not much. It...well, it looked much better before I fought with the man in the forest."

The father smiled and took the rabbit from her. "It will be more meat than we have eaten in weeks," the man said as he took it with a grateful bow.

"Is what you say really true?" the mother asked. "You fought the man? And then a tiger? What happened?"

Priya then remembered that the soldier had wanted to put a band of men together to go find and kill Nabhitha. "It is true," she said. "The tiger saved us. Please excuse me. I must try to stop the soldiers. I'll be back." She ran out of the hut and over to where the soldiers were gathering.

"Look alive, men!" the soldier was saying. "This tiger is apparently dangerous and has a taste for human blood. Keep your wits about you and shoot on sight!"

"Stop!" Priya said. "The tiger is not a threat to you. She only attacked the man because he was hurting me."

The man laughed. "You act as though you *know* this animal."

"I do," she said. "I've seen her before. We were on a ship together."

"I don't have time for a child's fanciful tales," the man said waving her off and turning away.

Priya grabbed his shoulder. "But it's true!"

The man turned and grabbed her wrist, squeezing it with so much force, she was nearly sent to her knees.

"Don't ever touch a British officer, you lowly ingrate," he sneered.

"Why should I be grateful?" Priya asked through the pain. "You seem to care more for some worthless rapist than justice."

The man released her wrist. "That man was a soldier in the Queen's army! I'll brook no slander against him without proof. We will find him and send him home for a proper burial, then dispatch his killer."

"My word is proof!" Priya said.

"Your word means nothing to me," the man said, then he turned away again back to his men.

"You can't—!" Priya started to say, but she felt a hand on her shoulder.

"You're only making this worse," a voice said.

Priya turned and gasped. It was the young customs official from the ship!

CHAPTER SIXTEEN

"You!" Priya said, her eyes wide.

His face grew from serious to smiling when she looked at him. His teeth showed, brightening his whole face, his eyes shining. He let out an awkward chuckle as though his words had left him.

Priya shook her head in shock, but she couldn't stop from smiling back and resisted the urge to hug him. It was so strange. She had only met him for a moment, and he had left her on the ship to be stolen away, but she was so happy to see a familiar face, even if it was one she had only seen after she had been kidnapped.

The man grabbed her hand and led her away from the bustle of the village center, behind the hut of the girl she had saved.

"You're alive!" he finally said. "And here! How? How did you escape?"

"You left me!" she blurted out. "How could you?"

His face fell and he shook his head in shame. "I know," he said, squeezing her hands tightly. "I haven't stopped thinking about that moment and hating myself for it. I will understand if you never forgive me. But you must know there was nothing I could have done."

Priya hated to admit it, but she knew he was right. She supposed it was why she wasn't angry with him.

"If I had protested anymore or tried to free you," he explained, "my commander could have tried me for insubordination and had me executed. If I had gotten off the ship at all. If the captain had pressed me into service, I might have ended up locked in a cage with you."

Priya nodded. She knew it was true.

"As it is, as soon as I got back to shore, my commander had me reprimanded and sent me here," the man said. "I'm just an infantryman again. I lost my position, my salary. I haven't even had a chance to figure out how to tell my mother. She's going to be so disappointed in me."

Priya squeezed his shoulder and gave him a reassuring smile. "She will be proud of you for speaking up."

He laughed. "I don't think you know my mother."

Priya chuckled. "Actually, I imagine she is a lot like mine. She thinks we should submit to the British in order to have some semblance of a safe life."

"And yet you ended up in the hull of a slaver's ship," the man said. "How did that happen?"

"It's a long story," she said.

"I wrote to your parents before I left Goa," he said. "I told them that you were alive and on a ship bound for America."

"Oh!" Priya gasped, her eyes watering. It was the first bit of good news she'd had since the disastrous meeting with the Evans family. "Thank you! Thank you so much!"

"It was the least I could do," he said softly. "I...I can't believe you are here. Thank the gods!"

"Jahangir!" a voice barked.

"Yes, sir!" the man said.

"What are you doing with that girl?" the commander asked. "There's a man-eating tiger on the loose! We need to get a move on! Report!"

"Yes, sir," the man replied and he started to follow after the soldier, but Priya grabbed his arm.

"What are you doing?" she asked. "You can't help them kill the tiger!"

"What?" he asked. "Why not?"

"Because she saved my life," Priya said. "That tiger..." She paused because she knew it was going to sound crazy, but it was the truth. "That tiger is my friend. We were on the ship together. We escaped together. We came to this village together."

His mouth dropped open. "Are you saying the tiger is tame?"

"Far from it," Priya said. "Nabhitha does only what she wants."

"What do you want me to do?" he asked. "They are getting a hunting party together."

"We have to stop them," Priya said.

"Jahangir!" the commander barked again.

"Yes, sir!" he said and tried to pull away from Priya, but she held fast to his arm.

"Jahangir!" she tied to say firmly, but it came out strangled. The man laughed.

"Zayn," he said.

"What?" she asked.

"My name is Zayn," he said. "Jahangir is my family name."

"Oh," Priya said. "Of course. Zayn."

"Look," Zayn said, gently gripping her arms. "I'll do

what I can to distract them or mislead them. But you need to stay here in the village where it is safe."

"But—" Priya tried to object, but Zayn finally pulled away and went to join the other troops. He looked back at her as he ran off, and she wondered if he immediately missed her as much as she missed him. She shook her head in confusion. Why did she miss him? They only just met. And he was just as submissive to the British as her parents were. He was not the sort of man she would ever be attracted to. Even if he was incredibly handsome. She couldn't see his hair because of the hat he had to wear with his uniform, but he had kind, gentle eyes and a strong chin with a dimple in the middle. When had she had time to notice that?

"Snap out of it," she told herself as she walked around the hut and watched the soldiers line up and head into the jungle, Zayn included. She didn't think they would ever find Nabhitha. Nabhitha was too smart to be caught by a bunch of dumb soldiers. Unless she put herself in harm's way by lingering around the village looking for Priya...She had been caught before, and perhaps because she had been protecting her cubs. What if she felt the need to protect Priya in much the same way? She felt anxiety rise in her chest, but she wasn't sure what to do. In fact, she felt a bit light-headed and her stomach ached. She then realized that she hadn't eaten in a while, and only had raw fish for days before that. She wandered back into the hut and her stomach growled and her mouth watered at the delicious smell of roasted rabbit.

The father walked over and led her to a low table. He then gave her a bowl of rice, a leg of the rabbit, and some boiled turnips. It was a poor meal, certainly, but Priya ate it ravenously, nearly brought to tears by how nourishing it was. She barely took a breath while she ate and ended up panting toward the end.

"You can take the rest of the rabbit with you on your journey," the father said with a smile.

"Thank you. And I...I'm so sorry," she said when she was finished as she wiped her mouth with the back of her hand. "I hadn't eaten for days."

"And you still found the strength to fight that terrible man?" the father asked.

Priya shrugged. "When I saw what was happening, I just got so angry that I had to do something." She looked up and saw that the man was looking at her with tears in his eyes. She looked around and noticed that the girl and her mother were not in the room. "Will she be all right?" Priya dared to ask.

The father nodded. "She is resting. Her mother refuses to leave her side. But she will be fine...in time." The man then had to pause as he wiped some tears from his eyes that he could not stop from falling. "Those damn British! I know who it was. He had been pestering my precious Chahna for months. She forced herself to be polite to him in passing, but she never gave him any indication that she would accept his advances—"

"I believe you," Priya said, cutting him off. "You don't have to explain it to me. He is—was—a bad man. He got what he deserved."

The man nodded, grateful for her understanding.

"Why are there so many soldiers here?" Priya asked. "Even in Bombay, I don't think I ever saw so many in one place."

"If you came from the beach, you wouldn't have seen

our rice fields," the father said, motioning toward the jungle. "We have harvested grains here for generations. Now, the British take most of the harvest in taxes."

Priya suddenly noticed how thin the man was. She also realized that he had not taken a bowl of rice for himself, and she remembered the rice that had burned while they were tending to the girl. Had that been their rice rations for the day? Did Priya just eat the only rice the family had to eat? She suddenly felt sick and terribly guilty.

"I'm so sorry," she said, pushing her bowl away. She reached for the rest of the rabbit and handed it to him. "Please, take it. Eat."

"No, no, no!" he said, shoving it back at her. "You deserve it after what you have done for us."

"I insist!" she said, shoving it back at him. "I had no way to cook it. Consider it payment for your hospitality."

"I couldn't," the man said, though she could tell his resolve was wavering.

"Please," Priya said gently. "Give it to your daughter if you won't take it for yourself. She needs her strength."

The man then burst into tears, no longer able to hold them back. "Blessed girl," he said, taking her hand. "I think the gods themselves have sent you to us this day."

Priya's eyes watered at the man's kind words and outburst of faith. She had no idea if the gods were behind her fateful journey or not, but she was glad she had been able to help the girl. She only wished there was more she could do.

"You will stay with us," the man said, clearing his throat and standing up. "For as long as you need a roof over your head, you can sleep here."

"You are too generous," Priya said, standing and clearing the table.

"Please excuse me," the man said. "I wish to check on my daughter."

"Of course," Priya said. "I'll just take a walk."

Priya then went outside, pulling her wrap around her shoulders as the sun set and coolness of evening settled in. There were many other villagers out this evening, enjoying the comfortable temperature. People were talking and laughing while children ran around playing. Priya's heart ached as she missed her own family. She was thankful to Zayn for letting them know she was alive. She wondered if there was any way for her to send them another letter letting them know that she was still in India and trying to get home. She doubted there was any kind of postal service in such a remote village. But as she traveled, she would surely come to a big enough town eventually. She remembered the gold coins in her bag. They would come in handy as she journeyed. She could use it to buy food. But not here. The villagers clearly needed all the food they had.

As she looked around, she realized that all of the people here were terribly thin. She thought about what the girl's father had said, about the British taking all off the village's grains in taxes. She then remembered the countless sacks of rice she had seen on the smuggler's ship. Anger burned in her once again at the cruelty of it. Fields and fields and fields of grains were grown and harvested by Indian families only for them to have to give it to the British for it to be shipped to a faraway land. In exchange for what? Protection? She didn't know any British soldiers who protected Indians. They raped Indians. They only protected British families.

Nabhitha did a better job of protecting Indians than the British. She then laughed at the thought. Maybe Nabhitha was a goddess in tiger form.

She then remembered that the soldiers were still out there hunting for Nabhitha. Priya narrowed her eyes and picked up a nearby torch. She marched into the jungle, determined to thwart the soldiers and save Nabhitha.

CHAPTER SEVENTEEN

*E*ven with her torch, Priya was not sure where in the jungle to go. Should she look for Nabhitha—as if she could ever find her—or the soldiers? Nabhitha would surely hide, while the soldiers would send her away if they saw her.

"This way, men!" she heard someone yell, so she followed the voice. "Keep your wits about you, men," she heard the man say as she got closer. It was the ranking commander. "A tiger is a dangerous predator. You probably won't even see her before she's got you by the jugular!"

"Shouldn't we wait until morning then, sir?" one of the men asked nervously. "I can't see a thing!"

"Nonsense!" the commander said. "We've got her on the run. Follow me!"

Priya didn't have much faith in the man's tiger stalking skills, but she didn't want to leave anything to chance. She started to follow the men at a distance when she felt a hand fall over her mouth. She tried to scream, but the man turned her to face him with his finger over his mouth, shushing her.

"Zayn!" she exclaimed.

"What are you doing out here?" he asked. "I told you to stay in the village."

"What are *you* doing to stop the soldiers from getting Nabhitha?" she asked.

"Just...I...you...I don't know!" he said. "I'm not a rebel like you. I do what I'm told. And how am I supposed to take on half a dozen men anyway?"

Priya exhaled in frustration. She knew that even together, they couldn't fight the soldiers. They needed to find another way to keep them from finding Nabhitha.

"We can't fight them," she said. "So we need a distraction instead."

"Like what?" he asked.

Priya looked around, but could see nothing other than trees and the fire from her torch.

"A fire!" she said. "We can set a fire. Then the men will have to work on putting it out and Nabhitha can escape."

"That...might work," he said. "But where? I don't think they will care if there is a fire in the jungle."

"Their barracks," she said. "They won't want to lose their possessions."

Zayn shook his head. "There aren't any. The men are being housed by the local families."

Priya grimaced at that. "That's terrible," she said, but she couldn't dwell on it. "Well, what do they care about?"

"The armory," Zayn said. "It doubles as a storehouse."

"You mean where they keep the grain before shipping it to England?" Priya asked. Zayn nodded. "I'd hate to destroy the food, though. The people here are starving. Have you noticed?"

Zayn blushed a little and nodded again.

"But still you serve in the British army?" Priya asked

incredulously. "How can you be a slave to them at the cost of your own people."

"I'm not a slave," he said firmly. "I have my own family to think about. My wages are guaranteed, which I need to support my parents and sisters."

"Didn't they just take your salary for speaking up on the smuggler's ship?" Priya reminded him.

"They slashed it, yes," he said. "But it is still more than I would make as a farmer."

Priya sighed in annoyance and turned back toward the village. "We can argue about this later. We need to steal the food, set fire to the armory, and save Nabhitha."

"I can't go with you," Zayn said. "The commander is already suspicious of you. If there is a mysterious fire, he will know it was set by you. If I'm not around when the fire starts, he will surely suspect me too since he has seen me talking to you."

"Then come with me," she said. "We can run away now. Tonight. It would be safer if we traveled together anyway."

"I...what?" he asked. "Run away? To where?"

"I need to get home," she said. "Back to Bombay."

"But what about me?" he asked. "What about my family?"

Priya shrugged. "I don't have all the answers. But I know what I'm going to do. You can either come with me or run back to your commander."

"Priya," he said, and her name rolling off his tongue nearly caused her heart to melt. "What you are asking is impossible. I've already lost so much."

Her heart went out to him. She reached out and dared to touch his cheek with her hand. His skin was warm and soft.

"I know you have," she said, and she meant it. She

understood that he was conflicted. "But whether you come with me or not, I'm going."

She then turned away and hoped he would follow her, but she knew he wouldn't. He was too much like her parents. He had invested too much in holding up the status quo, living by the rules the British had put in place. If he stood against the British, he and his family would suffer. Priya had already lost everything and was not afraid to lose more. While she desperately wanted to get home, she knew that her parents already thought she was lost to them. They wouldn't be any worse off if she died tonight. But she had to help Nabhitha. She had lost track of how many times Nabhitha had saved her life. Plus, she could help the villagers too. They needed that food. She would sneak it away to the families and they could hide it. Then, after Priya set fire to the armory, the soldiers would think that the food was destroyed in the flames. It was a perfect plan.

Until it wasn't.

Priya had thought that all of the soldiers had gone to hunt for Nabhitha, but she was wrong. As she rounded the armory, she came face to face with one guard that had stayed behind, and he had a rifle.

"Hey! What are you doing here?" the soldier asked.

Priya's hand went to the knife in her belt. Her mouth went dry and she licked her lips. Could she do it? Could she really kill someone?

"What's that?" he asked, pointing to her belt.

Priya turned and tried to run away. She couldn't do it! But she felt a hand on her shoulder and he spun her around. She pulled out her knife and slashed, cutting the man's arm.

The man groaned in pain and let her go as he reached for his arm. "What the hell?" he asked.

Now what? Priya thought. She needed to decide now! But she was frozen. Any choice seemed like the wrong one.

"Hey!" another voice called out. The soldier turned around and promptly fell backward. Priya looked up and saw that Zayn had punched the man in the face, knocking him out cold.

"You need to stop picking fights with men bigger than you," he joked.

Priya felt a flood of relief wash over her, but it didn't last long.

"Come on!" she said as she ran into the armory, Zayn right behind her. The armory was little more than a one-room hut. One half of the room stored the soldier's weapons —guns, knives and swords, grenades, and small barrels of gunpowder. One spark could easily blow the whole thing up. In the other half of the room were countless bags of rice.

"Get rid of that torch," Zayn ordered. Priya turned around and tossed it to the ground outside of the hut. It was too dangerous to have it inside the armory until they wanted it to blow. "Hold out your arms," he said. He then loaded up one, two, then three bags of rice. They were so heavy, she thought her knees were going to buckle under the weight, but fear of getting caught kept her going.

"Go, go, go!" Zayn said. He tossed two more bags of rice out of the hut, then he grabbed the torch and tossed it back inside. "Run!" he told her as he picked up the bags. They both ran toward the hut where the family lived and didn't even look back as they heard the explosion behind them.

Everyone in the village screamed and many ran toward the fire with the hopes of putting it out. They didn't want the whole village to catch on fire.

"What's going on?" the girl's father asked as he opened the door and Priya and Zayn ran inside.

"Do you have somewhere you can hide these?" Priya asked, indicating the bags of rice.

"By the gods, girl, did you steal those?" the father asked.

"I liberated them," Priya said breathlessly. "Hide them, and then distribute them discreetly among the other villagers. The soldiers will think they were destroyed in the fire."

"What fire?" the father asked as he put his head back out the door. "Oh, that fire."

"What is going on out here?" the mother asked as she emerged from the back room.

Priya exhaled in annoyance. "You need to hide these bags of rice," she said.

"We need to go!" Zayn said. "The soldiers have returned. They are focused on the fire, but it is already going out."

"Please!" Priya nearly screamed.

"U-u-under my daughter's bed," the mother said. "I don't think the soldiers will dare disturb her for a while after what happened."

"Thank you," Priya said as she rushed into the room and shoved the bags under the bed.

"What's happening?" the girl asked as she sat up in her bed, shaking with fright.

Priya ran her hand down the side of the girl's face. "Nothing you need to worry about," she said. She wished she could stay longer, but she knew they needed to go. She ran back to the main room and grabbed her bag. She pulled out two gold coins and gave them to the father. "For your troubles," she said.

"I couldn't!" he started to protest, but Priya stopped him. There was no time to be polite.

"I must insist," she said.

"We will pray for you," the mother said as Priya and

Zayn ran out the door. They ran past another hut, and Zayn ducked inside. He ran out with his pack already prepared.

"When did you have time to do that?" Priya asked.

"A soldier is always ready," he said. He then grabbed her hand and they ran down the trail that led through the jungle and back to the beach. The jungle was too dark and treacherous to try and traverse at night. On the beach, they would have the light of the moon and a relatively uncluttered path.

Priya saw that the soldiers were all still gathered around the armory, but the fire was nearly out. She hoped that Nabhitha had time to escape. As they ran down the jungle path, she looked behind her and saw a streak of orange dart across the trail and she smiled. Nabhitha was safe and was following her.

Once they got to the beach, they didn't have time to take in the beauty of the ocean crashing on the shore at night. They kept running. If they wasted any time, the soldiers could easily catch up with them. As exhausted as they were, they ran all night.

CHAPTER EIGHTEEN

$\mathcal{F}$inally, as the sun rose over the sea, Priya and Zayn had to slow down. They stopped for a moment and sat on a piece of driftwood to catch their breath. Zayn reached into his pack and pulled out some dried meat and his canteen. He handed both to Priya.

Priya accepted them gingerly and felt more than a little foolish. She realized she had been too hasty. She should have made some preparations before going to the armory. She didn't pack any clothes or food or refill her canteen.

"Thank you," she mumbled as she ate and drank. She only took a small amount before handing them back to him. It didn't feel right, taking his rations.

"You know, seeing you in the light of day, I think I may have been too quick to run away with you," he said with a smirk.

Priya gasped and her hand flew to her hair. She then remembered the clunky boots she was wearing and her makeshift sari.

"Well, you try surviving a shipwreck and see what you look like," she replied.

Zayn chuckled and shook his head as he looked out at the sea. "I still don't know how you did that."

"It was Nabhitha," Priya said. "I was drowning. I can't swim very well. She swam alongside me and dragged me to a longboat. Then she let me ride on her back as she swam us to shore."

Zayn laughed, but then he noticed Priya was serious. "You...you are telling me the truth?"

Priya shrugged. "I have no reason to lie to you. I know it sounds crazy, but it is the truth. We protected each other on the ship, then she saved me and I kept her alive by catching fish."

Zayn shook his head. "You are amazing," he said. "Like Durga."

"What's Durga?" Priya asked.

"You know," he said. "The goddess. She rose out of the sea on the back of a tiger to vanquish the evil. She is fearless."

"Fearless?" Priya asked. "Like Nabhitha." She remembered that she called Nabhitha by that name because the sailors had called the tiger fearless. How strange the world was.

"You would know better than I," he said.

"Maybe Durga is my personal goddess," Priya said. "My mother will be glad to know that." Once she got home, she would have to learn all she could about Durga and give her thanks.

Zayn then stood up. "We should keep moving," he said. "We need to stay well-ahead of the soldiers."

"How far is Bombay?" she asked.

"Very far," he said. "We are north of Goa, but not far north enough. Maybe we can procure a horse somehow."

Priya wondered if she had enough gold to buy a horse.

She hoped she did. She wanted to get home as soon as possible. Then she would tell her parents about Lord Fullerton. She didn't know if her word alone would be enough for him to be arrested for kidnapping, but she hoped it was.

"Why did you help me?" she asked Zayn after they had resumed walking for a bit.

Zayn shrugged but didn't offer an answer.

"Tell me," she said.

"You won't like my answer," he said. "You want me to say that I came to my senses and did the right thing. Or that I couldn't be away from you. But those would be lies."

Priya blushed. She knew that she was attracted to him, but she didn't think he would be developing any feelings for her. They'd only just met! It would be crazy for him to throw his life away for her so soon.

"Then what is the real reason?" she asked. "I know you better than you think. You follow the rules and do as you're told."

"After I just saved your life," Zayn said, "you continue to insult me?"

"I'm just stating the facts," she said. "If you think that is an insult, well, that says more about you than me."

"Hmm," Zayn said. "Maybe. But the truth is, I realized I would be blamed for the fire whether I helped you or not. The British, they say that we Indians have the right to serve in the army, but they don't really want us there. They will use any excuse to demote or discharge us. I was already there as a punishment. If you were successful in your attempt to destroy the armory and get away, the commander would want someone to blame. And that someone would be me."

"I'm sorry," Priya said.

"For what?" Zayn asked.

"For involving you in my mess," she said. "I...I must admit that I don't think Indians should be supporting the British Empire, especially the military. But I also don't think I have the right to force people to act the way I want them to. I didn't mean for you to end up a runaway and losing everything and having no way to support your family. If you wanted to take the risk on your own, I'd be very glad. But I'm sorry you were forced into this life."

"I'm not a runaway," Zayn clarified. "I'm a deserter. A traitor."

"What do you mean?" Priya asked, suddenly alarmed.

"I deserted my post," he said. "And I attacked my fellow officer. And I sabotaged the armory. If I'm caught, I'll be executed."

Priya stopped walking and her heart caught in her chest. "What?" she nearly shrieked. "Executed? Why didn't you tell me?"

"I knew what I was doing," he said stonily. He turned to look at her as she stood planted to her spot. "Priya, I appreciate your passion. This fire that motivates you. But you need to understand what you are truly asking of people when you tell them they need to rebel against the British."

"I...just...things could be better..." she stammered.

"Perhaps," he said. "But do you know what will happen to that family if the rice is found in their home?" Priya didn't respond. She didn't want to know the answer. "I don't regret what I've done, Priya. But, in the future, be careful who you ask to go on this journey with you."

Zayn resumed walking, but Priya looked down at her feet, her face full of shame. She knew his words were not meant to wound her, but they still stung. In her fury, she had put many lives at risk, and she was sorry for that. She only hoped there was some way to atone.

"Zayn!" she called out as she ran up to him. He looked back and her and couldn't suppress a smile. She was panting when she caught up with him. "I...I just want to say—"

"Seize them!" a voice barked.

Priya and Zayn looked up in shock as Zayn's commander and the other soldiers came running out of the jungle toward them. Three men went straight for Zayn. Zayn tried to fight back, but he was quickly overpowered.

"No!" Priya screamed as she ran over and pummeled one of the men on the back with her tiny fists. The man turned and backhanded her across the face, sending her to the ground.

"Stop!" Zayn said as two men grabbed him by the arms and forced him to his knees. "Don't hurt her. She's innocent. I'm the one you want."

"You are the deserter," the commander said. "But she is no innocent."

The man who Priya had cut with the knife stepped forward, half of his face black and blue from where Zayn had punched him.

Priya jumped to her feet. "I knew I should have killed you!"

"You don't have it in you," the commander said.

"Just watch me," Priya said through gritted teeth as she stomped toward the commander.

The commander laughed as two more men grabbed Priya by the arms and forced her to her knees as well.

"You know, I rather like you in that position," the commander said with a lick of his lips.

"Don't you touch her!" Zayn yelled, but one of the men

punched him in the stomach, knocking the breath out of him.

"Shut up, both of you!" the commander ordered. "By the authority vested in me by Her Majesty the Queen, I hereby sentence both of you to death."

Priya gasped. How could this be happening? After all she had been through! All she had survived! She was so close to going home! Her eyes scanned the tree line, looking for Nabhitha. *Please, please, please,* she begged silently, but she didn't think the tiger would save her this time. There were too many men and they had guns. Nabhitha was no match for them.

The commander motioned to one of the men. "On your mark."

"Sir!" the man said as he stood in front of Zayn and held his rifle up.

Priya screamed. "Please, no! Stop!"

"Look away, Priya," Zayn said as he pulled his arms free from the men who were holding him and sat up straight.

"I'm sorry!" she yelled. "I'm sorry! Please, God! No!"

The crack of a rifle rang out in the air and Priya screamed again. But Zayn didn't fall. There was no smoke coming from the soldier's rifle.

Then the soldier sank to his knees and fell on his face.

"What the devil?" the commander yelled.

A chorus of yelling rang out as several Indian men ran out of the jungle, shooting rifles and swinging swords.

Priya and Zayn were immediately forgotten as the soldiers and the Indians clashed. Bodies on both sides fell. Priya had no idea what was going on, but she knew this was their chance to escape. She made her way through the fray toward Zayn. But a soldier got between them. Zayn grabbed the barrel of the man's rifle with his hand, aiming it away, and then punched the man in the face, sending him to the ground. Zayn took the rifle and turned toward Priya.

"We need to run," he said.

There was suddenly more screaming as a ferocious roar rang out. Priya looked toward the jungle and saw men moving aside, dropping their weapons and running away as Nabhitha headed straight for Zayn.

Priya saw that Zayn had the gun pointed at her. Nabhitha must have thought that Zayn had intended to hurt her. Priya jumped in front of Zayn and held her arms out.

"Nabhitha!" she screamed. "No!"

Nabhitha stopped in her tracks, panting hard. She chuffed at Priya, but then lowered her head and growled at Zayn.

"He's a friend," Priya said. "He saved me." Nabhitha did not seem so sure and remained in her attack pose. "*Lower your gun*," Priya whispered to Zayn.

"Are you crazy?" he asked. "She's going to eat me."

"Lower it if you want to live!" Priya ordered.

Zayn dropped the gun, and immediately, Nabhitha's mood changed. She raised her head and took a step back.

Priya looked around and saw that the men who were still alive on the beach were staring at them in shock.

"Run!" Priya told Nabhitha. "Go!"

Nabhitha did as she was told and fled the beach back into the jungle.

Zayn dropped to the ground, his hand over his chest. "I...I thought I was dead."

Priya sighed in relief. "So did I," she said. "I really didn't know if she would stop or not."

Then they laughed.

"She is a goddess!" someone said.

Priya looked back at the other men and saw that the Indian men were on their knees bowing to her. The few British soldiers who were still alive ran off into the jungle.

"No, please," Priya said, suddenly embarrassed. "I'm nothing. Please don't."

"Oh, Goddess Durga," the men chanted, "who rose from the sea to vanquish evil, I bow to her, I bow to her, I bow to her again and again."

CHAPTER NINETEEN

*P*riya ran over and grabbed Zayn's arm. "Come on!" she said. "We need to go. These people are crazy!"

Zayne stood up. "Go where? The soldiers caught up with us. More will come. We need a plan."

One of the men who attacked the soldiers stood up and indicated that the rest of the men should stand too. They stopped prostrating themselves and went to work scavenging for supplies from the fallen soldiers.

"Please, do not leave," the man said, holding out his hands in a sign of friendship. "What you just did...I'm sorry, we were so overcome with emotion. Come, join us."

"Us?" Zayn asked. "Who are you?"

"My name is Krish Bakshi," the man said. "My men and I have been fighting against the British for months. I don't know who you are, but when I saw the soldiers try to kill you...Well, any enemy of the British is a friend of ours."

The other men laughed and Priya held Zayn's arm tighter, giving him a tug signaling that she still wanted to leave.

Zayn gave her a small nod. "We thank you for your assistance," he told Krish. "But we should get moving. More soldiers will come for us and we just want to get home."

"You won't outrun them," Krish said. "We found their horses tied nearby. That was how they caught up with you. If more will come, as you say, you will still die this day without our protection."

"Is that a threat?" Zayn asked through gritted teeth.

"On the contrary," Krish said. "It is an offer of friendship. Please, you look tired, hungry. We have food, water, and can offer you protection from the soldiers. Believe me, I would not threaten the girl who can control a tiger." He smiled at Priya.

As Priya met the man's gaze, she relaxed a little. She did not sense any malice from him. And even though she did not control Nabhitha, it didn't hurt that he believed she did.

"*I think we can trust him,*" Priya whispered to Zayn.

"*Are you sure?*" he asked her. "*We don't know anything about him.*"

"*But we can't keep running,*" she said. "*We need help.*"

Zayn nodded and then turned back to Krish. "Thank you for your offer, friend. We will follow you."

"Wonderful!" Krish said. "Come with me." He turned and walked back toward the jungle, waving for the other men to follow. They all smiled at Priya when she caught their gaze, but she did not feel threatened by them. They seemed to look at her as a friend or daughter, not a piece of meat they would devour if given the chance.

In the jungle, they came across half a dozen tethered horses. Krish took the reins of one and handed it to Zayn.

"As our honored guest, please take one," he said. "I would not have the goddess's feet touch the ground for longer than necessary."

"I'm not—" she started to say, but Krish cut her off with a laugh.

"Deny it all you want," Krish said. "But I know what I saw."

Priya pressed her lips but did not protest further. Surely Krish knew that she was only a girl. But he seemed to think it was hilarious when he made her angry, so she bit her lip.

Zayn climbed up on the horse with ease and then offered his hand to Priya. Her eyes went wide and she stepped back. "I can't ride that."

"I won't let you fall," he said, and her heart fluttered. She took his hand and he lifted her up on top of the huge beast. She nearly fell over the other side as she tried to find her balance, but he reached out and placed his hand on her waist. "Hold on to me," he said.

Priya wrapped her arms around his chest, pressing herself against his back. She could feel his heartbeat under her hands, a calming steady rhythm. She sighed as she took in his scent, his warmth.

The other men mounted the rest of the horses and they all took off at a slow pace through the overgrown jungle. They eventually came to a narrow path, and the horses were able to pick up speed. Priya worried that Nabhitha would not be able to keep up with them, but then she thought she heard a low, almost imperceptible growling emitting from the trees, so she was sure Nabhitha was nearby.

The light filtering through the trees cast shadows across her face that flickered by at an irregular beat. She closed her eyes and laid her head on Zayn's back. She was warm and felt safe, and the shadows seemed to have a hypnotizing effect on her. Somehow, she soon fell asleep.

*T*he sounds of laughter and chatting awoke her sometime later. She blinked a few times as they entered what looked like a makeshift village. The huts were actually British military tents. Priya thought that Krish's men had stolen them. But there were not many, maybe ten, and they were all situated around a central bonfire. There were a few goats and chickens milling about. She saw a couple of women and children, but most of the people were men. As they entered the camp, she noticed that there were many men with guns standing around the perimeter.

The riders stopped and dismounted the horses, Priya and Zayn following suit. One of the men came along and gathered the horses to lead them out of the small camp.

"Welcome to our humble home," Krish said, and Priya gave a polite nod of thanks.

"This is not a village," she said. "What is going on?"

"Oh, the British burned my village," Krish said matter-of-factly. "Killed my family and dozens of others. Most of the people here are survivors from villages the British have destroyed."

"What?" Priya nearly shrieked. "Why? Why would the British do that?"

"It's a long story," Krish said. "Well, each of us has a different long story. It always begins innocent enough. People taxed to the brink of starvation, princes and magistrates stripped of power or position, children indoctrinated at the schools to betray their families and beliefs. One thing leads to another until the British kill everything you love and you end up here."

Priya shook her head in disbelief. She knew that the British laws were cruel and taxing, but she didn't know that they were going around murdering whole villages of people. As much as she hated the British, she almost couldn't think that badly of them. She looked at Zayn and saw that his face did not show the level of shock and outrage hers did.

"Did...did you know about this?" she asked. When he didn't respond, she punched him in the arm. "Did you take part!"

"No!" he said, flinching. "I...no. I was just a customs official until a week ago, you forget. But even then...I knew what was happening. I'd heard stories."

"And you did nothing?" she screeched, punching him in the arm again.

"Priya," he said pleadingly, shaking his head. She knew what he meant. It was "complicated." Her head knew that, but she was still angry about it. But he was here now, so she couldn't stay mad at him for long.

"I do not blame you, my friend," Krish said to Zayn. "The British have been here for two-hundred years. We should have asserted ourselves a long time ago. But now, the way things are has become such a part of our lives, it is difficult to get people to see the need to fight back until they have lost everything."

"That is what you are doing?" Priya asked. "Fighting back?" Her hopes lifted. They really were rebels! These might be the people she had been searching for. People like her who were ready and willing to take India back from the British.

Krish laughed. "We are mostly a minor annoyance, causing trouble for the soldiers when and where we can. But something big is coming."

"What?" Priya asked, her eyes sparkling.

"Wait, goddess," he said. "Patience. We will speak more tonight. But first, rest, wash, eat. My home is your home."

At that, two of the women approached and led Priya away. She watched as some of the men offered Zayn a cigar and led him in another direction. The women took her behind a large muslin cloth that had been draped on a rope where there was an old metal wash bin filled with water. They helped Priya undress and get into the tub. They used soap to wash her clean, and for the first time in weeks, her skin was no longer caked with salt. They poured buckets of water over her head and used their fingers to comb through the tangle of knots. When she stood up, she was embarrassed by the muddy water she left behind, but the women just laughed. They knew the struggles of living in the jungle and near the beach. They gave her a new clean sari and choli to wear and burned the rags she had been wearing. It was yellow, much brighter than she normally would be comfortable wearing, but the clean silk was so soft on her skin she didn't dare refuse. One woman gave her a handwoven slouch bag she could use to carry her few precious items. They then brushed and oiled her hair and plaited it tightly.

One woman pulled out a small jar of cocoa butter and ran it over the scars on Priya's arm. She told them about her time on the ship and how Nabhitha had left her mark on her as a warning and a reminder.

"The girl with tiger stripes," the woman uttered. Priya remembered that the ship's captain had once called her the same thing.

"No wonder the men all think you are a goddess," one woman said with a laugh. "And they don't even know about you escaping from the shipwreck."

"Please don't call me a goddess," Priya said, rubbing her

arm. "I'm just a stupid, idiot girl who got herself kidnapped. I never should have left home."

The other women giggled or tisked and sighed shaking their heads.

"We know you are not a goddess," one of the women said. "But you are brave. You are strong. You have survived so much. We need a woman like you among us. A woman who can show other women and girls that they can fight back too."

"You fight with the men?" Priya asked, intrigued.

"I do!" one woman who appeared to be middle-aged said with pride. "If I have an arm, I can raise a sword."

"But most of us support the men in other ways," a younger woman said. "They need food, their wounds need tending. We all play our part."

"But only British men fight," the older woman said. "If only Indian men fight, there are not enough. But if all of us were to raise a fist against them, we could drive them off in a day. Right into the sea!"

Priya laughed at that, but there was a ring of truth to it. Indians outnumbered the British by the millions. How had India even ended up in this situation? Priya sighed. She knew she would never know the answer to that. As Krish had said, the British had been in India for two hundred years. This dynamic had been building for centuries.

One of the women then brought Priya some food. Fresh naan, curry, and goat cheese. All thoughts of rebellion fled Priya's mind as she dropped to her knees and devoured the food. She tried to apologize, but she was completely incomprehensible with her mouth stuffed with food. She was nearly brought to tears as she ate her fill.

"Calm yourself, child," the older woman said, squeezing

Priya's shoulders. "We will make sure you never go hungry again if you stay with us."

"Stay?" Priya asked when she finally slowed her eating. She had become so excited by the rebels' cause, she had forgotten that she had been on a journey to get home. "I don't know."

"You must!" the other women said. "Please!" they begged.

Priya finished her meal and stood up. "My parents. They think I am lost to them forever. I need to let them know I am safe."

The older woman nodded. "I understand. There is a city about half a day's ride from here. I am sure we could send a letter to them from there."

"That would be wonderful," Priya said. "I could go tomorrow."

"Oh, I don't think so, child," the woman said. "I heard you are running from soldiers, and that many were killed on the beach. It would be very dangerous for you to leave the camp right now."

"But—" Priya started to object, but the woman had led Priya back to the middle of camp. When she saw Zayn, her words left her.

He had also been washed and fed and given new clothes. He looked years younger. He gave her that heart-melting smile and everyone and everything seemed to fade away.

The woman squeezed Priya's shoulders, momentarily bringing her back. "Why don't you and your friend talk about what you should do. Then listen to what Krish has to say. I am sure you will make the best decision." She gave Priya a mischievous smile as she walked away. Priya wondered if the woman had been a village matchmaker before she became a rebel.

"You look..." Zayn paused as he tried to find the right words. "Like a girl," he finally settled on, and Priya felt the smile flee her face, which made Zayn laugh. "You must know you looked like you had just crawled out of the sea before."

"Well...yeah. I did," she said. "I feel like myself for the first time since I was kidnapped. I don't even know how long ago that was, but it feels like years."

Zayn nodded. "You've been through a lot," he said. He motioned for her to walk with him. They went past the tents to walk around the perimeter where they could have a little privacy. "I can understand if you want to keep heading home."

"I do," she said. "But with the soldiers still looking for us, it might be too dangerous to try and leave now. Krish might not let me."

"Krish will not hold you against your will," Zayn said quickly, and Priya raised an eyebrow. "He and I have been talking and I like what he has to say. Things are coming to a head quickly. The time to act is upon us."

"But what is different?" Priya asked. "Why now?"

"This might be the first you are hearing about rebels," Zayn said. "In the cities, I am sure your information is limited. But different villages and communities have been rebelling against the British for years. But without any way to organize, the British usually put the rebellions down quickly, killing anyone who would speak against them. And they don't allow the newspapers—British or Indian ones—to report on them. But now, the country is changing. People are more mobile. There are trains and telegraphs and a postal service. Survivors have been able to share their stories and drum up support. Krish is mounting an army. This camp is only one of many hidden throughout the region. They are only waiting for his signal to strike."

"What signal?" Priya asked.

"I don't know," Zayn said. "He wouldn't tell me. But he is holding a camp-wide meeting tonight. I think he wants to tell everyone at the same time. Whatever it is, I want to be a part of it."

"Look at you," Priya said, beaming. "And I thought you were just a toadying soldier boy."

"I think you will want to be a part of it too," Zayn said, stopping and taking her hand. Her heart thumped hard in her chest. "I want to thank you for bringing me here."

"Zayn..." she started to say, but her words fled.

"I mean it," he said. "I know I resisted following you at first. I was scared. But I was so unhappy before. Just standing by while my countrymen were having everything taken from them. So many sold as slaves."

Priya gasped.

"Yes," he admitted, his eyes rimmed red with shame. "You were not the first person I saw in the hull of a ship who had been kidnapped. There were many, many others. When I think about what they must have suffered—"

"Zayn," Priya said, reaching up and stroking his face. "It's not your fault. You couldn't have stopped it. You spoke up for me and still couldn't save me."

"I'll never forgive myself for that!" he said gripping her arms. "I couldn't protect you then, but I will protect you from now on."

"I'm safe now," she said. She could feel her entire body burning for him. The intensity of his gaze was pure fire, and she wanted to go up in flames.

Zayn pulled her up to him and placed his lips on hers.

She reached around his head and gripped his hair. He backed her into a tree and opened his mouth, taking in her lips, her tongue. Every inch of her body tingled and ached for him. She groaned as he kissed her chin and her throat. Then she gasped as he did the unthinkable and squeezed her breast.

"Priya...Priya," he panted as he pressed against her. She felt his hand inch up her sari to her waist. She wanted him. Her heart and her body wanted this man.

But not like this. In the woods against a tree. On the run, starved and exhausted. Exposed in the woods where anyone could walk upon them at any moment. She wanted him, but she wanted to lay in his arms all night until the sun rose. She wanted him to take his time exploring every inch of her. She remembered her grandmother's wedding sari and how it had been her dream to wear it on her own wedding day. Which made her think of her mother and how ashamed and disappointed she would be in her.

"No," she finally whispered, gripping his wrist.

"What?" he asked.

"No," she said more clearly. "Not...not like this."

He moved his hands to her face and kissed her again, but with less force. "A goddess deserves better," he said softly.

"Don't call me that," she said, pushing him away.

He chuckled, but as he turned away, he froze. Priya looked up and saw that Nabhitha was watching them. She was not growling or purring, but was just sitting, watching, her tail flicking back and forth.

"I think she was just making sure you weren't hurting me," Priya said.

Zayn raised his hands and backed away slowly. "I'll,

uhh...I'll see you at the meeting with Krish." He slipped through the tents and back into the camp.

Priya then looked back at Nabhitha and crossed her arms over his chest. "You scared him away. Are you happy with yourself?"

Nabhitha stood and walked back into the jungle without a look back.

CHAPTER TWENTY

*P*riya took a moment to calm her breathing and straighten her sari before following Zayn back into the camp. By the time she got there, everyone had already gathered around to hear what Krish had to say.

"—time has come!" he was saying as Priya walked in and everyone clapped and cheered. Krish saw her and smiled. "Even the gods and goddesses have smiled upon us."

She rolled her eyes and everyone laughed. She locked eyes with Zayn on the other side of the crowd. He smiled and she blushed, looking away so she could focus on what Krish was saying.

"Now is the time for action. The time to fight back. To take back India!"

The crowd erupted into cheers and Priya clapped along, feeling pride swell in her heart. She was glad to be here, to be part of this moment she was sure was going to be important in the history of India's long march toward freedom.

"And I know how we are going to do it," Krish said, and everyone held their breath. "We are going to kill the governor."

Everyone gasped and started talking at once. Priya's hand went to her mouth. Did he really just admit that he was going to murder—assassinate—the governor?

The governor was the queen's emissary in India, and he acted with the full authority of the British Crown. He was practically the king of India, though governors tended to change every few years—usually because they grew so wealthy so quickly they saw no reason to stay. The current governor was the Viscount Canning. Other than his name, Priya knew very little about him.

Krish motioned for everyone to quiet down. "I know this seems shocking, but it is very simple. The governor is traveling with his family from Bombay to Goa overland instead of by sea so he can assess the land and give encouragement to the local British officials. He is traveling with an armed contingent, of course. But we have more men than he realizes. We also have the element of surprise. We can swoop in and kill the governor and anyone who stands in our way and slip away before anyone even realizes what happened. This will be an act that the British government will not be able to keep quiet. Once the rest of India knows that we were successful, everyone will be empowered to stand up! To fight!"

The crowd erupted into cheers again, but Priya was horrified. She couldn't believe Krish's grand plan was to murder the governor, and he would be traveling with his family. Were they going to be killed too? But then Priya realized that she had been a fool. Did she really think an armed open rebellion would not end in bloodshed? She had already seen Krish and his men kill soldiers on the beach. She should have known that Krish's "something big" would involve more killing.

She shook her head and tried to slip out of the crowd.

She wanted to get to Zayn and run away before anyone noticed. She couldn't be part of this.

But Krish saw her. "Goddess!" he called out. "Will you join us?"

She turned toward him and the crowd went silent, waiting for her response in anticipation. She knew what they wanted her to say. She only hoped they would not turn on her when she disappointed them.

"No," she said. She had expected the crowd to erupt in angry jeers, but they just stood stone silent as they looked from her back to Krish.

"Why not?" he asked her.

"I'll not condone murder," Priya said.

"It is not murder when it is in self-defense," Krish challenged. "Was it murder when your tiger killed the man in the woods?"

"That's not the same thing," Priya said. "The governor is not a rapist or a murderer. I'm not his judge or executioner."

"Every bag of grain he exports to England is just like taking food from the mouths of our children," Krish said. "Every child who dies of hunger is a life on his hands."

"But what about Canning's children?" Priya shouted. "You said his wife and his children are with him. Presumably there are other friends and servants traveling with them as well. They are innocent in all this. But if you attack their caravan, they could die too."

"There are no innocents among the British," Krish said, and most of the crowd seemed to agree with him. "Every person who eats Indian rice, or wears Indian silk, or drinks Indian tea contributes to the exploitation of the Indian people."

The crowd clapped in agreement. Priya looked for Zayn, but she could not see him.

"Every man or woman who wants to fight," Krish said, "come to me for your assignment. Everyone else, plan to break down the camp and travel to meet at the rendezvous point afterward. Get ready for a war!"

The crowd erupted into cheers again and began to disperse. Most of the men went to Krish, as did some of the women. A few people gathered in other areas to discuss how they were going to move the camp.

Priya tried to slip away, but she was approached by some of the women from earlier.

"Won't you fight with us?" one of them asked.

"The girl with the tiger would be quite a fright!" another exclaimed.

"No," Priya said, trying to get away. "I can't be part of this."

"But you are part of it," the first woman said. "The soldiers won't stop looking for you. You should join us to strike while you have the element of surprise."

"I won't be party to murder!" Priya said, growing frustrated. Why wouldn't they just let her leave?

The other women crowded around her, one grabbing her by the arm and shaking her.

"They have murdered us for hundreds of years!" someone shouted, then other angry voices joined in around her.

Priya tried to pull away, but she couldn't. She closed her eyes and covered her ears. She just wanted to go home...

"Let her go!" Zayn's voice cut through the angry voices and they quieted. Zayn wrapped his arm around Priya's shoulder and moved her away from the crowd. "No one should be forced to fight against their will."

Some of the women continued to argue with him, but Priya walked away out of the camp, making her way toward where the horses were being kept. She wrapped her arms around herself and rubbed her hot cheeks. How had she come to be here? What was going on? Should she try to return home alone? Warn the governor? Move with the camp? She wanted to support the rebels' cause, but committing murder was a line she couldn't cross. What should she do?

"Priya!" Zayn called out as he trotted up to her. "What are you doing? Aren't you going to join Krish?"

"No!" Priya nearly shrieked. "How can you even consider it? This is crazy! It's wrong. We can't be party to this. We need to leave."

"And go where?" Zayn asked with nearly a chuckle.

"Home!" she said. "I have only ever wanted to get back home."

Zayn shook his head. "*You* can go home," he said. "But what about me? I have a family, yes, but the army will be looking for me. If I go back, I'll be caught and could put the rest of my family at risk for harboring a deserter, a fugitive, a traitor!"

"Come with me," Priya said. "We will figure it out later. We can find you a new name. A new life. No one in Bombay will know who you are. Just come with me."

"You are just going to leave?" Zayn asked. "After everything you have been through? This is your chance to be part of something greater. A chance to avenge all of India. I thought that was what you wanted. I'm here because of you."

Priya shook her head and turned away. "I...I didn't know!"

"Didn't know what?" he asked, placing his hands on her shoulders.

"Anything!" Priya yelled turning back, her eyes watering.

"I didn't know anything about life or death or rebels or killing. I didn't know you. I didn't know I would miss my mother so much. I'm...I keep saying I'm just an idiot girl who ran away. This was all a mistake."

Zayn smiled and cupped her cheek in his hand. "You are not an idiot girl," he said. "You are the girl with tiger stripes. You just don't know it yet."

Priya reached up and took his hand in hers. "Don't do this," she begged. "If the governor or his family are killed, the British will never stop hunting you until you are dead."

"My life is already forfeit," he said sadly. "I'll fight until the bitter end, but it might not be so bitter with you at my side."

Priya's heart swelled. She wanted to stay with him. Fight with him. Protect him. But she couldn't. She almost chuckled at the wild rebel he had morphed into from the straight-laced British toady he was only a few days before. She had done that to him. Perhaps she held more power than she realized.

"I can't," she whispered.

Zayn pressed his lips and nodded, his disappointment clear on his face. He lifted her chin and placed a gentle kiss on her lips. "Farewell, tiger girl." Then, he turned and walked away back into the camp.

Priya reached up and wiped the tears from her cheeks that she didn't realize had fallen. She heard a low rumbling and knew Nabhitha was watching her.

"It's just you and me again, girl," Priya said. "What should we do?"

Nabhitha stepped out of the jungle and into the light. She lifted her head and sniffed the air. Then she let out a low growl.

"You can sense it, can't you," Priya said. "The danger in the air. This is going to end badly. I know it."

Nabhitha grunted and shifted on her feet as though she was anxious about something.

"We need to leave, no question about that," Priya said. But what she left unsaid was that she also needed to do more. It felt traitorous to say it out loud, but she wanted to warn the governor of what was coming. If the rebels lost the element of surprise, maybe Krish would call off the attack. She could save the lives of the governor and the rebels.

"Come on," Priya said as she untethered a horse and climbed up on its back. "We can't just let this happen."

She led the horse to the trail that would lead to the road toward Bombay. If the governor and his men were heading toward Goa, that is the road they would be on.

CHAPTER TWENTY-ONE

*P*riya had been so lost in thought as she rode that she came upon the governor's traveling party sooner than she expected. She knew it was the governor not only because the camp was much bigger than the one she had just left, but it was far more well-apportioned. There were plenty of lanterns, not merely torches, and the tents were new and large. There were also dozens of armed guards standing around. From inside the camp, she could hear voices of laughter and music playing. The family must have brought a phonograph with them. She rolled her eyes at the thought of being able to travel with such frivolous items when she didn't even have extra clothes or enough food to eat.

But frivolity was not a reason to die. She had to somehow warn them that the rebels were coming. She tied her horse to a tree and walked toward the camp. She heard Nabhitha let out a low growl, but she waved at the woods to indicate she would be okay. She hoped Nabhitha understood. She raised her hands as she approached the guards.

"You there!" a voice rang out. "Freeze!"

Priya lowered her eyes and held her hands higher. "I'm unarmed," she said. "I'm here to deliver a message for Governor Canning."

One of the guards lowered his gun and stepped toward her, twisting her arm behind her back. Another guard kept his gun trained on her.

"A message?" the guard who held her arm asked. "From who?"

"I can only tell the governor that," Priya said.

"How about I lock you in a cage for a few hours?" the guard said, gritting his teeth at her. "Or worse."

"It's a matter of life and death," Priya said. "It's about Krish."

The guard looked at his companion. "Who's Krish?" the other guard asked.

"That rebel who's been giving us trouble," the first guard said. He then shook Priya's arm. "What do you know about him?"

"I can only tell the governor," she said.

"If you're lying—" the guard growled.

"I'm not lying," she said, looking him in the eye now. "But if you don't do as I say, people will die."

The guard hesitated for a moment, then he spoke to his companion again. "Stand guard," he said. "She could be a decoy. I'll take her to the governor and get to the bottom of this." The guard then took her into the camp, to the central tent where most of the voices and the music were coming from. There were more guards here. Priya looked around and tried to guess how many armed men there were. She lost count, but knew there were far more guards than rebels in Krish's army. Krish might have the element of surprise, but as soon as the shock wore off, the soldiers would certainly have the upper hand.

The guard then took Priya through the flap of a tent and her eyes widened at the opulence of the room. There were bright lights, plush carpets, heavy wooden furniture, and crystal goblets. It looked like a proper British sitting room, not a tent in the middle of the jungle. There were many children sitting on the floor playing with toys and adults sitting around drinking and socializing while a lively tune emitted from the phonograph. Priya had to shake her head to remind herself that she wasn't dreaming. She heard several gasps as she was dragged into the room.

"What's all this?" a balding man with a long, pointed nose like a bird's beak asked as he stood and walked over. Priya thought he must be Viscount Canning, the governor.

"This girl says she has a message for you, m'lord," the guard said.

"Well, it must be quite interesting to interrupt my evening over," Governor Canning said. Priya felt her throat go dry. Now that she was here, she wasn't sure what to say. She never thought in her life she would come face to face with the governor himself. "Come now, out with it," he insisted.

"You need to leave," she finally squeaked out.

Governor Canning cupped his hand around his ear. "What was that?" he asked.

"You need to leave," she said again more clearly. "You are in danger here and you need to leave."

The governor frowned and furrowed his brow. He looked back at the guard and Priya noticed that one of the women had her arms around her children with a worried look on her face. The other British people left with their children, presumably to go to the comfort of their own tents.

"What is she babbling about?" the governor asked the guard.

"She said something about Krish," the guard said.

"What?" the governor said loudly. "If you know something about that blaggard, girl, I demand you out with it."

Priya's heart raced. She was in the center of danger. While Krish might have protected her as best he could from the British, this man was not her friend. He would do whatever it took to get information out of her and then he would probably thank her by executing her as a traitor. It had been a mistake to come here, but what could she do now? She heard one of the children whimpering and she shook her head. She had to follow through with her plan now, no matter the consequences.

"Krish is planning an attack," she said. "He's coming. You and your family need to leave here. Now!"

"The devil..." Governor Canning said, running his hand over his mouth. He turned and paced for a moment, as though debating what to do. "No," he finally said. "No, we stay here. We will not be cowed by that rabble-rouser."

"Reports say that rabble-rouser was responsible for the massacre on the beach, sir," the guard said. Priya tried to school her face. She couldn't let them know that she had been there when the soldiers were killed. "If he's coming, he could pose a real threat to you and your family. We should leave."

"No," the governor said.

"Charles!" the woman with the children said, jumping to her feet.

"No!" the governor said to her more firmly, then he turned back to the guard. "If we leave, we will be more vulnerable on the road. Here we can set up blockades, put up more lights, arm more guards. We will be safer here."

The woman sank to her seat and shook her head, holding her children to her even more tightly.

"It will be alright, my love," the governor told her, giving a weak smile, but she did not seem convinced. He turned back to the guard. "Well, what are you standing around for? Get to work on fortifications. We need to be ready for anything."

"Yes, sir," he said. "But what about the girl?"

Governor Canning looked at her as though he had forgotten she was there. "Did you check her for weapons?"

"I'm unarmed," Priya said. The governor gave the guard a nod, who then ran his hands over her body, his hands giving her bottom a squeeze before announcing that she was indeed unarmed.

"She's not a danger," the governor said. "Go."

"Sir," the man said with a quick bow as he let go of Priya and left the room.

"So, how did you come across this information," the governor asked her.

"I...came across his camp. Heard him telling his men his plans," she said, but she knew her voice was unconvincing.

"You just *happened* to come across the camp and just *happened* to get close enough to hear his plans without him seeing you?" the governor asked, his eyebrow raised. "Come now, tell me the truth. Are you part of his little band of merry men?"

"No," Priya said. "I don't follow Krish. But I believe some of his complaints against British rule are valid."

"But, my dear," he said patronizingly. "Without us who would protect you from such violent ruffians?"

"We wouldn't have rebels if the British weren't burning Indian villages," Priya said. The governor stared at her, stone-faced, and Priya wondered how she had found the courage to speak so bluntly to a man of his station. But as she looked at him, his collar loose, his wife looking at him disapprovingly, she realized he was only a man like any other.

The governor then chuckled. "A girl as young as you cannot possibly understand the complexities of the situation."

Priya crossed her arms. He was clearly trying to dismiss her, but she would not be ignored. "I understand enough to be kidnapped and sold as a slave. To see people starving and girls raped at the hands of British soldiers." Canning's wife gasped and covered her children's ears.

"That's enough," the governor said. "You've upset my wife quite enough for one evening. What is it you want? I suppose this information about Krish does not come for free."

"I want you to leave India," Priya said. "All of you. Every last British person who has set foot on our land."

The governor laughed. "You know that isn't going to happen, child."

"Not today," Priya said. "But one day India will belong to Indians again."

"And in the meantime?" the governor asked. "What do you want now?"

"To go home," she said. "I need to go home."

The governor nodded. "If you survive the night, I'll see to it that you are released."

"You can only do that if you survive the night too," Priya said.

The governor opened his mouth to make a retort, but he was interrupted by the sound of gunfire. Everyone gasped and the children cried. The governor turned to comfort his family and Priya took her chance to escape. She turned and ran out of the tent.

She expected the camp to be in chaos, but it wasn't. The camp was mostly empty. The guards were all stationed at the perimeter working like a well-oiled machine.

"Aim! Fire! Aim! Fire!" she could hear the commanders calling out over and over again. She could hear screaming and grunts of pain, but they were mostly coming from beyond the line of soldiers. Krish's men. Her own countrymen were dying. Zayn! He was out there.

She ran through the camp, looking for a break in the line of guards so she could escape, tell the rebels to pull back. They couldn't fight the soldiers, not like this. She finally saw a small skirmish break out. Some of the rebels had gotten close enough to the soldiers to fight them hand to hand and disarm them. But even without weapons, the soldiers were mostly superior fighters.

But that was when she saw Zayn. He ran forward toward one of the soldiers, a sword held high. He punched and kicked a soldier, knocking him down and running him through with his sword. He then raised his sword and motioned for others to follow him. Several rebels ran forward, including Krish and some of the women. They ran at the soldiers along the line, trying to take more of them down.

Priya then heard a high-pitched squealing noise. She realized one of the soldiers was blowing a whistle, signaling the other soldiers that they had been breached. She looked back and saw that several soldiers were running across the camp toward the rebels.

"No!" Priya yelled, running toward Zayn. "Fall back! Fall back! They are coming!"

Zayn and Krish looked up and saw her. But instead of retreating, they both charged forward.

The soldiers in the camp dropped to their knees and raised their guns.

"Aim!" the commander yelled.

Priya's heart froze as she watched Zayn running straight for the guns.

"No!" she screamed.

"Fire!"

Shots rang out. Followed by screams. A flash of orange. And then a deafening roar.

Priya felt something large knock her to the ground. She looked up just in time to see Nabhitha charge into Zayn, sending him to the ground as well. Several of the rebels fell back, clutching their stomachs or chests. The soldiers had the advantage, but when Nabhitha stood between the guards and the rebels and roared, the guards took off at a run. Nabhitha started to run after them.

"No! Nabhitha!" Priya yelled as she scrambled to her feet and ran to Zayn's side. "Are you hurt?" she asked him. Zayn shook his head. He wasn't injured, but he was clearly stunned. "Then let's get out of here!"

Priya ushered him to his feet and called to Nabhitha, urging her back to the jungle. Priya and Zayn then ran to Krish, each of them grabbing one of his arms and helping him back to the jungle. They and the other rebels went to where they had tied the horses. They helped as many of the injured as possible onto the horses, then the rest followed behind on foot as they made their way through the jungle to where the rebel camp had moved.

*T*hey made it to the camp by the time the sun rose. They then helped the injured and counted how many were missing, most likely dead.

"You warned them we were coming, didn't you?" Zayn finally dared to ask Priya when they found a moment alone. "That's why you were there in the camp."

Priya shook her head. "I couldn't do nothing," she said softly. "I thought that if Krish realized he had lost the element of surprise, he would call off the attack."

Zayn nodded. "He should have," he said. "We saw that the camp was far more fortified than it should have been. I told him we needed to pull back, try another night. But he was insistent."

"Why?" Priya asked. "Why did he do this?"

"I don't know," Zayn said. "It was all for nothing. If not for you, for Nabhitha knocking me out of the way of the guns, I could be dead now too."

"He's asking for you," one of the rebels said, coming up behind them.

Priya hesitated. She wasn't sure she could face Krish. She had betrayed him. Ruined his rebellion. If he died, he would be right to blame her. But Zayn placed his hand on the small of her back, urging her forward. At least she wouldn't be going alone. She gulped and walked into the tent where Krish lay dying.

Krish held his hand out to Priya as she entered. She ran to him, kneeling by his side and taking his hand. "I'm sorry!" she cried. "I didn't mean for any of this to happen."

Krish placed his other hand on the back of her head. "It is I who should apologize," he said. "In my pride, I thought it would be me who led our people to freedom. But it was never me. It was...another..." He grunted and exhaled sharply. Then his head fell back on his pillow.

"Krish!" Priya said, shaking him. "No! Don't leave us! We need you!"

"Priya," Zayn said, wrapping his arms around her.

"No!" Priya cried. "No, no, no..." She then turned and sobbed into Zayn's chest. "Why? Why is this happening?"

"It's not your fault," Zayn said.

Priya pulled away from him and paced the room. "What did he mean? Another?"

Zayn stood and shrugged. "He is gone. The rebels need another leader. He must have thought it was you."

"No," Priya said, her tears fleeing. "No. I can't do something like that. I...look at what I caused! I wanted to help my people, now half a dozen of them—and Krish—are dead! The smuggler is dead. The soldiers on the beach are dead. Oh my God. I just leave a trail of dead bodies everywhere I go. If you don't leave me, Zayn, you'll be next!"

"Priya," Zayn said, gripping her shoulders and giving her a little shake. "Calm down. None of this is your fault. You are stronger than you know. Stay with us. Help us. With you and Nabhitha, we can do anything."

"Nabhitha?" Priya asked. She pulled away from Zayn and looked around. Where was the tiger? Of course, Nabhitha wasn't in the tent. Nabhitha had saved Zayn and ended the battle. She must be in the jungle, watching, waiting, like a fierce mother protecting her cubs.

Priya thought about her own mother. How she always was so calm in the most trying of situations. She always had a word of warning, always did her best to guide Priya in the right direction. But Priya had always fought back. Always pushed her mother away. Now, she wished more than ever that she had the wisdom of her mother to help her. She needed to go home. But there was something she needed to do first.

"Goodbye, Zayn," Priya said as she moved toward the tent's flap.

"What?" Zayn asked, grabbing her wrist. "Where are you going?"

"I have to go home," she said. "I need to speak to my mother. I need her help. Her guidance."

Zayn released Priya's wrist and nodded. "You will always have a place with us."

Priya reached up and caressed his face. "We will see each other again. But I have to do this."

Zayn nodded and Priya flew out of the tent before she could change her mind. She grabbed a horse and jumped onto its back. She turned it toward the road to Bombay. She looked out to the jungle and smiled as she saw a flash of orange.

She needed to see her mother, but she needed to save Nabhitha's baby first.

CHAPTER TWENTY-TWO

$\mathcal{A}$s Priya rode into Bombay, it was dark, and fat raindrops were falling on her intermittently. In the distance, thunder rolled. It wasn't storming yet, but it would be soon. Good, she thought to herself. A heavy rainstorm would provide good cover for her and Nabhitha as they searched the Evans' house for the tiger cub.

The area where the Evans and the Parkers lived was on the eastern edge of the city, away from the port but encroaching on the jungle. Still, they had to pass through several neighborhoods of varying styles to get where they needed to go. Priya watched in awe as Nabhitha crept through backyards and over shanty houses completely undetected in order to follow her.

Priya stopped outside the Parker house and tied her horse nearby. She felt a tugging in her heart, urging her to go inside. She was home, finally! After nearly being shipped to the other side of the world, she was back where she started. Her poor parents must certainly be worried sick about her. But if she went inside, she knew they would not let her leave to save Nabhitha's baby. It wouldn't take long.

She would slip inside, find the cub, give it to Nabhitha, and then return home. She took a deep breath and forced herself to walk away from the Parker house and down the street to the Evans home.

She approached the house cautiously. Even though it was late at night, there would still be people awake to stand guard and alert the night watch if necessary. She watched as Nabhitha sniffed the air and then began to shuffle her feet anxiously. She had never been here before, but it was as if she knew this place. Priya thought that Nabhitha must be able to smell her baby. Priya let Nabhitha take the lead. Nabhitha would be able to get them into the house and find the cub. Priya would only be there to keep Nabhitha from hurting any of the home's residents.

Nabhitha paced by the gate to the backyard. The yard where the fateful garden party had been held weeks before. Priya walked over and tried to open the gate, but it was locked. Nabhitha sat back on her haunches and then leaped over the gate as though she were flying!

"Nabhitha!" Priya hissed, unsure how she was going to follow. She grabbed the gate and pulled herself up, using the latch as a foothold. She made it to the top, but as she hauled herself over to the other side, her sari caught on it, tangling her leg. As she crashed down to the ground, she heard her sari rip and felt her leg tear. She hit the ground hard and stuffed her fist in her mouth to keep from cursing. She sat up to survey the damage. Thankfully she hadn't broken anything. She took off her shoulder wrap and wound it around her leg to staunch the bleeding. She forced herself to her feet and to ignore the pain. She then unlatched the gate and pushed it open slightly so she and Nabhitha could make a quick getaway.

By the time she caught up with Nabhitha, she was on

the back porch, peeking in the windows looking for a way in. Priya made her way up the steps and to the back door. She tried the door handle, but it was locked as well. Nabhitha nudged Priya out of the way and placed her paw on the handle. With her massive paw, she broke the handle sheer off the door. It clattered to the ground, and Priya heard the other half of the handle hit the floor on the other side as well.

"Shh!" Priya said, realizing how dumb it was to try and explain to Nabhitha the importance of being quiet. Nabhitha nudged the door open with her nose and slipped inside, sniffing the air. Priya stepped in behind her just as a servant came running down the hall toward them with a knife.

"Thieves!" the man called out, but Nabhitha hissed at him, lowering her stance and laying her ears flat. The man froze in terror, dropping the knife to the floor.

"We won't hurt you," Priya said. "We are just looking for the baby tiger. This is the cub's mother."

"S-s-s-second floor," the man stuttered. "The boy's room."

"Thanks," Priya said. "Now get out of here, but tell no one what you saw."

"Yes...yes!" the man said as he backed up and then ran out the front door. *Good*, Priya thought. *Another way to escape.*

Nabhitha stalked her way through the house. Priya followed her, but winced as she put weight on her leg. She looked back and saw that she was leaving a trail of blood. She needed to get home soon before she passed out from blood loss. She picked up the knife the servant had dropped, just in case.

Nabhitha slinked up the stairs to the second floor and

went straight to a room at the end of the hall. She reached up with her paw to break the door handle again, but Priya stopped her. She knew this door wouldn't be locked, so no sense making more noise than necessary. She opened the door and followed Nabhitha inside.

For it being night, the room was bright. Everything was white, reflecting the moonlight coming into the room through the large windowed door that led to a balcony. As soon as they entered, the kitten began mewling uncontrollably. Nabhitha ran to it and began chuffing to comfort it.

"Please, be quiet," Priya whispered to them both, but it was no use. The kitten was in a small cage that Nabhitha could not open, but she was so anxious to get to her baby, she would hardly move aside to let Priya help.

"Kitty!" a small voice called out.

Priya looked up and was horrified to see that the little boy had woken up and was crouched at the end of his bed watching them.

"Shh!" Priya said, but she could hear Nabhitha growl. Priya turned back to fuss with the latch to get the tiger cub out, but then the light to the room flipped on.

"What the devil?" a man's voice bellowed. A woman screamed.

Priya looked up and saw Sahib and Memsahib Evans standing in the doorway of the child's room.

"My gun!" the man yelled. "Get my gun!"

"No!" Priya yelled. Nabhitha roared and stalked toward them. The man ran from the room, probably to find a weapon, but the woman would not leave her child.

"Get back!" the woman screamed feebly at Nabhitha, but Nabhitha bared her teeth and screeched.

Priya finally jumped up between them.

"You!" the woman gasped. The boy jumped off his bed

and ran to his mother. She picked him up and held him tightly.

"Did you think I was dead?" Priya asked. "When you left me at the port, I bet you never thought you'd see me again."

"I...I didn't know it was you.... I didn't recognize..." the woman stumbled with her words.

"Is that what you told my parents?" Priya said. "You would face down a tiger for your child, but did you laugh when you saw how heartbroken my parents were for me? Or when you took the baby tiger away from its mother? Are we all just animals to you?" Priya placed her hand on the back of Nabhitha's head as the tiger stalked forward.

"P...please," Memsahib Evans begged as she stepped back into the hallway. "I...I'm sorry. I'll do whatever you ask."

"Leave," Priya said, holding up the knife. "Leave India. You've done enough damage here already. Leave my country and never return."

"Yes," Memsahib Evans said, nodding her head quickly. "Yes, we'll go." She then backed down the hallway, never taking her eyes off of Priya until she reached the stairs. Then she was gone in a flash.

Priya turned back around, feeling a little woozy, but she held it together long enough to run back to the baby tiger's cage. She unhooked the latch and pulled the cub out. Nabhitha snuffled and licked the baby, who mewed happily.

Priya then heard angry voices from downstairs. Priya ran over and shut and locked the door. "We don't have much time," she told Nabhitha. "That must be the night watch."

She went to the glass doors and threw them open. She didn't see a way down from the balcony other than to jump. Nabhitha stepped out and looked down. She then looked up at Priya.

"It's okay," Priya told her. "Go. I'll be fine. You have your baby. Get her to safety."

Nabhitha picked up her baby in her mouth then leaped from the balcony to the ground below. She stumbled, but then caught herself and ran toward the fence, leaping over it with ease. She looked back at Priya one last time. Priya waved, and then Nabhitha was gone. And Priya knew that this time, she was gone for good.

Priya turned around, feeling dizzy and nauseous. She slipped and saw that she was standing in a puddle of her own blood. She fell to the ground just as two men broke the door down and entered the room.

"Drop the weapon!" the men said.

Priya had forgotten she was holding a knife, which she immediately let go of.

"Help me," she mumbled. "Take me home."

"Arrest that little monster!" Sahib Evans yelled. "She tried to kill us."

"Help me," she mumbled as the men took hold of her. "Help me. Amma!"

CHAPTER TWENTY-THREE

*P*riya awoke to the sounds of shouting. She groaned and placed her hand on her head. She opened her eyes and saw the Evans, the Parkers, several police officers, and her parents all standing around yelling at each other.

"Amma!" Priya cried out, and when her mother ran to her, she could not stop the tears from flowing.

"Priya!" her mother wailed as she held her daughter tight. She then felt her father's arms around her as well.

"See," Sahib Evans said. "She's awake. Now arrest her."

"Calm down, Evans," Sahib Parker said. "The girl has clearly been through a terrible ordeal."

"Does that excuse attempted murder?" Sahib Evans sneered.

"How dare you make such accusations against my daughter," Priya's father said, standing up.

"I'm sure Priya didn't try to murder anyone," Memsahib Parker said, playing the peacemaker.

"My daughter is injured," Amma said. "She needs a doctor."

"I'm fine, Amma," Priya said, not wanting to incur such a cost. "I just need to rest."

"What happened?" Lucille asked, kneeling down beside her. "When you went missing, we were so distraught."

"Did you tell them where I went?" Priya asked.

"Umm...no," Lucille said, biting her lower lip nervously. "I...I didn't want you to get in trouble."

"Were you protecting me or yourself?" Priya asked.

"Priya!" Amma gasped, giving her daughter a warning glance. Priya then looked around the room and realized that —in their way—the Parkers had been defending her. Protecting her against the accusations of the Evans. If Priya didn't want to end up in jail, she needed to play nice with the Parkers—for now.

"I...I'm sorry," Priya said, closing her eyes, her hand flying to her forehead again. "I'm just so tired. I feel sick."

"Of course," Priya's mother said. "Can we please take her home now."

"Yes," Sahib Parker said before anyone else could speak up. "I don't know what happened, but no one was seriously hurt, right, Evans?"

"She broke into our home," Sahib Evans went on. "Stole our son's pet. Waved a knife at my wife. To say nothing of the deadly tiger!"

"This is crazy talk!" Memsahib Parker said. "A tiger? Really. You must have been dreaming."

"I know what I saw!" Sahib Evans roared.

"Let's go!" Memsahib Evans said as she headed for the door. "These people are never going to believe us. It's too dangerous here. We are going to pack our things and go home."

"Oh, darling," Sahib Evans said, following her. "You can't mean that."

"I do!" she said. Then she looked at Priya, and Priya gave her a hard stare back. A look of understanding passed between them. Memsahib Evans gave a curt nod. "I do," she stated again. "We are leaving this dreadful place." She then left the house, her husband quick on her heels.

"Well," one of the officers said. "If Mr. Evans doesn't press charges, there's nothing more to be done here. I'll bid you a good day, sir." He gave Sahib Parker a nod and then he and the other officer left.

Everyone who was left breathed a sigh of relief when the door shut. Memsahib Parker then sat in a chair near Priya.

"I thought they would never leave," she said much too cheerily. "Priya, we are so glad you are home safe. But where have you been all this time?"

Priya looked at Lucille, still worrying her lower lip. She then looked at Sahib Parker and thought she saw sweat on his brow. Did he know about Fullerton? If he did, would she be safe if she spoke out? She looked at her parents, tears still hanging on the edges of their eyes.

"I...I need to talk to my parents," Priya finally mumbled. "I'm just so glad to be home."

Memsahib Parker nodded. "I understand," she said. "Take all the time you need."

Priya then looked around and realized that she was in the Parkers' house. She didn't know why she didn't recognize it before. Her head must have still been fuzzy. She swung her legs off the couch she was reclining on and winced as she tried to stand on her injured leg. Her father picked her up and carried her out of the house, her mother following closely behind. They all crossed the backyard and went into their little cottage.

Her father took her to her bedroom while her mother busied herself making chai. Priya settled into her own bed and deeply breathed in the scent of the tea when her mother brought it to her. Her mother then unwrapped her leg and set about washing it. Priya could see that the wound had already been washed and wrapped at least once. Her mother must have taken care of it while she had been unconscious. Her mother then opened a jar of ointment and slathered it over the wound.

"Hopefully your leg will not scar the way your arm has," Amma said.

Priya glanced down at her arm. She had become so used to the marks on her arm that Nabhitha had left there, she didn't really think of them as scars anymore, but as badges of honor.

"Would you believe me if I told you I got those marks from a tiger?" Priya said with a smirk, but her mother did not smile.

"Where have you been?" Amma asked.

"I was kidnapped," Priya said.

"Kidnapped?" Amma asked, surprised.

"Didn't you get a letter telling you?" Priya asked.

"It only said that you were on a ship bound for America," Appa said, sitting in a chair nearby. "We thought you had run away."

"I..." Priya paused, trying to remember everything that had happened. The details were becoming fuzzy. Or maybe that was the blood loss. "I did hope to find work somewhere else, but I never would have left without talking to you about it. I went to see a man named Lord Fullerton. He promised honest work. Lucille sent me to him. But when I got there, he drugged me. I woke up as I was being taken onto a smuggler's ship."

"Lord Fullerton?" Amma asked, sending her husband a worried look.

"Yes," Priya said. "Why? Do you know him?"

"Priya," Appa said. "You must never tell anyone about this."

"Why?" Priya asked. "He needs to be arrested. According to Za...a customs official I met, countless Indians are still being transported to the slave markets around the world. We need to stop him."

"No, Priya," Amma said, exasperated. "Lord Fullerton is powerful, and a friend of Sahib Parker. If we want to keep a roof over our heads, you will never speak of this."

Priya's jaw dropped. She couldn't believe what she was hearing. "I...I thought I was going to die," she said. "That I would never see you again. I was nearly raped. Almost drowned. But I was a lucky one. All those people who have been sold into slavery are lost forever. I could have been one of them. We can stop this. We need to speak up. It is time to do something."

"No," Appa said. "Now is the time to be quiet. Be loyal. There is talk of rebellion everywhere. The British are nervous. They are sending more soldiers. If anyone is suspected of being disloyal, they are immediately fired. Do you want us to end up on the street?"

"I want us to stop letting the British treat us like animals," Priya said. She then reached into her sari and pulled out the coin purse she had managed to keep safe all this time. She handed it to her mother. "This can take care of us for a while."

Amma gasped when she opened the bag. "Where did you get all this?" she asked.

"From the smuggler's ship," Priya admitted. Amma

handed it to her husband. "How much do you think it is?" Priya asked.

"A lot," he said. "But not enough to feed us for the rest of our lives. This might get us by for a while, but then what?"

"Maybe by then things will be different," Priya said. "If the rebels are successful—"

"They won't be," Appa said, cutting her off and putting the money in his pocket. "And I'll allow no more talk of rebels."

"So, what now?" Priya asked. "I'm back and everything is just the same as it ever was?"

"Yes," Appa said. "I must go to work, and so must your mother. You rest. When you are healthy, we will look at getting you a respectable job again."

"Oh, Appa," Priya said shaking her head. "Don't you see? Nothing will be the same again."

Appa sighed but left without another word.

"Amma," Priya said, gripping her mother's arm as she moved to leave. "You can't think that nothing has changed."

"I can hope it," Amma said as she cleared away the tea things and then left the cottage.

Priya shook her head at the absurdity of it. Did they really think they could just go back to the way things were? She forced herself out of bed and over to the window. She watched as her mother smiled and laughed as she played with the Parker children.

Her parents were right. Here, nothing had changed. Priya had changed. She had seen too much. Experienced too much. She ran her fingers over the scar on her other arm. The changes were deep and permanent.

She had to leave.

She couldn't stay here and pretend nothing had

happened. Pretend that India wasn't a powder keg waiting to blow. Something was going to happen, and she wanted to be part of it. Zayn had said she would always be welcome with the rebel army. She didn't agree with all of Krish's tactics, but with Zayn as the leader and Priya by his side, she could help the rebels fight back, but perhaps in a morally superior way.

She went to her room and found paper and a pen. She began to write a letter to her parents. She would leave, but she would not be so impetuous as before. Her leg was injured and she was still hungry and exhausted. She would heal, then she would pack a bag with food, clothes, and anything else she could think of. She would tell her parents where she went and why so that they would not need to worry. She would let them keep the gold coins so she wouldn't have to worry about them.

She would leave. She would join the rebels. She would fight.

She would become the girl with tiger stripes.

The End

THANK YOU

Thank you for reading A Girl and Her Tiger! If you enjoyed it, I hope you will leave a review. If you want to know when the next Animal Companions adventure is released, be sure to join my mailing list!
http://zoeygong.com/subscribe/

ACKNOWLEDGMENTS

I would like to thank my friend, author Lom Harshni, for answering all my questions about Indian life, culture, and history, and pointing me in the right direction on several issues.

If you would like to know more about India under British rule, I highly recommend the book *Inglorious Empire: What the British did to India* by Shashi Tharoor.

A GIRL AND HER ELEPHANT

books2read.com/elephantgirl

One girl risks everything to save the life of her friend...

All of the elephants wept as one of their own lay dying in childbirth. But Kanita, the daughter of the royal elephant trainer, refused to give up. With her own hands, she helped bring the baby elephant, Safi, into the world, beginning a lifelong friendship between a girl and her elephant.

But many of the villagers worried about the curse of the white elephant with the red birthmark across her face.

Raised in the mountains of northern Siam, Kanita's idyllic life is shattered when she is ordered to marry a much older man and leave her beloved yet cursed elephant behind. But Kanita's stubborn nature refuses to bow to her parents' wishes.

Kanita and Safi flee their village with the goal of redeeming Safi from her cursed reputation and cementing their bond, vowing to never be separated.

But the jungle is more dangerous than Kanita or Safi could have imagined.

Follow Kanita and Safi through the jungles of ancient Siam in a story of friendship, hope, and redemption.

A GIRL AND HER PANDA

books2read.com/pandagirl

Lihua never could have imagined that the birth of a little brother would end the life she knew.

Raised in a poor country village, Lihua prayed her parents would have a son to bring peace and balance to the family. But she did not foresee how living in such poverty would force her parents to face a terrible choice they once made that would now cost Lihua everything.

Suddenly told to leave her home, Lihua begins a treacherous journey alone. After being attacked on the road the first day, an unlikely hero comes to her aid: a panda she decides to call Panpan. Bound together for love and survival, Lihua and Panpan travel together through the mountains and forest of western China as Lihua struggles to find her new place in the world.

ABOUT THE AUTHOR

ZOEY GONG was born and raised in rural Hunan Province, China. She has been studying English and working as a translator since she was sixteen years old. Now in her early twenties, Zoey loves traveling and eating noodles for every meal. She lives in Shenzhen with her cat, Jello, and dreams of one day disappointing her parents by being a Leftover Woman (剩女). Learn more at ZoeyGong.com.

f facebook.com/ZoeyGongAuthor

g goodreads.com/zoeygong

BB bookbub.com/authors/zoey-gong

ABOUT THE PUBLISHER

*VISIT OUR WEBSITE
TO SEE ALL OF OUR HIGH QUALITY BOOKS*:

http://www.redempresspublishing.com

**Quality trade paperbacks, downloads, audio books, and books
in foreign languages in genres such as historical, romance,
mystery, and fantasy.**

www.ingramcontent.com/pod-product-compliance
Lightning Source LLC
Chambersburg PA
CBHW020633180626
46816CB00003B/938